AFRICAN WRITERS SERIES FOUN

Novels are unmarked
*Short Stories
†Poetry
‡Plays
§Biography/Politics

PETER ABRAHAMS
6 *Mine Boy*
CHINUA ACHEBE
1 *Things Fall Apart*
3 *No Longer at Ease*
16 *Arrow of God*
31 *A Man of the People*
100 *Girls at War**
120 *Beware Soul Brother*†
THOMAS AKARE
241 *The Slums*
TEWFIK AL-HAKIM
117 *The Fate of a Cockroach*‡
T. M. ALUKO
11 *One Man, One Matchet*
30 *One Man, One Wife*
32 *Kinsman and Foreman*
70 *Chief, the Honourable Minister*
130 *His Worshipful Majesty*
242 *Wrong Ones in the Dock*
ELECHI AMADI
25 *The Concubine*
44 *The Great Ponds*
140 *Sunset in Biafra*§
210 *The Slave*
JARED ANGIRA
111 *Silent Voices*†
I. N. C. ANIEBO
148 *The Anonymity of Sacrifice*
206 *The Journey Within*
253 *Of Wives, Talismans and the Dead**
KOFI ANYIDOHO
261 *A Harvest of Our Dreams*†
AYI KWEI ARMAH
43 *The Beautyful Ones Are Not Yet Born*
154 *Fragments*
155 *Why Are We So Blest?*
194 *The Healers*
218 *Two Thousand Seasons*
BEDIAKO ASARE
59 *Rebel*
KOFI AWOONOR
108 *This Earth, My Brother*
260 *Until the Morning After*†
MARIAMA BÂ
248 *So Long a Letter*
FRANCIS BEBEY
205 *The Ashanti Doll*
MONGO BETI
13 *Mission to Kala*
77 *King Lazarus*
88 *The Poor Christ of Bomba*
181 *Perpetua and the Habit of Unhappiness*
214 *Remember Ruben*
STEVE BIKO
217 *I Write What I Like*§
OKOT P'BITEK
147 *The Horn of My Love*†
193 *Hare and Hornbill**
YAW M. BOATENG
186 *The Return*
DENNIS BRUTUS
46 *Letters to Martha*†
115 *A Simple Lust*†
208 *Stubborn Hope*†

AMILCAR CABRAL
198 *Unity and Struggle*§
SYL CHENEY-COKER
221 *The Graveyard Also Has Teeth*†
DRISS CHRAIBI
79 *Heirs to the Past*
J. P. CLARK
50 *America, Their America*§
WILLIAM CONTON
12 *The African*
BERNARD B. DADIE
87 *Climbié*
DANIACHEW WORKU
125 *The Thirteenth Sun*
MODIKWE DIKOBE
124 *The Marabi Dance*
DAVID DIOP
174 *Hammer Blows*†
MBELLA SONNE DIPOKO
57 *Because of Women*
82 *A Few Nights and Days*
107 *Black and White in Love*†
AMU DJOLETO
41 *The Strange Man*
161 *Money Galore*
T. OBINKARAM ECHEWA
168 *The Land's Lord*
CYPRIAN EKWENSI
2 *Burning Grass*
5 *People of the City*
19 *Lokotown**
84 *Beautiful Feathers*
146 *Jagua Nana*
172 *Restless City**
185 *Survive the Peace*
BUCHI EMECHETA
227 *The Joys of Motherhood*
OLAUDAH EQUIANO
10 *Equiano's Travels*§
MALICK FALL
144 *The Wound*
NURUDDIN FARAH
80 *From a Crooked Rib*
184 *A Naked Needle*
226 *Sweet and Sour Milk*
252 *Sardines*
MUGO GATHERU
20 *Child of Two Worlds*§
FATHY GHANEM
223 *The Man Who Lost His Shadow*
NADINE GORDIMER
177 *Some Monday for Sure**
JOE DE GRAFT
166 *Beneath the Jazz and Brass*†

BESSIE HEAD
101 *Maru*
149 *A Question of Power*
182 *The Collector of Treasures**
220 *Serowe: Village of the Rain Wind*§
LUIS BERNARDO HONWANA
60 *We Killed Mangy-Dog**
TAHA HUSSEIN
228 *An Egyptian Childhood*
SONALLAH IBRAHIM
95 *The Smell of It**
YUSUF IDRIS
209 *The Cheapest Nights**
OBOTUNDE IJIMÈRE
18 *The Imprisonment of Obatala*‡
EDDIE IROH
189 *Forty-Eight Guns for the General*
213 *Toads of War*
255 *The Siren in the Night*
KENJO JUMBAM
231 *The White Man of God*
AUBREY KACHINGWE
24 *No Easy Task*
SAMUEL KAHIGA
158 *The Girl from Abroad*
CHEIKH HAMIDOU KANE
119 *Ambiguous Adventure*
KENNETH KAUNDA
4 *Zambia Shall Be Free*§
LEGSON KAYIRA
162 *The Detainee*
A. W. KAYPER-MENSAH
157 *The Drummer in Our Time*†
JOMO KENYATTA
219 *Facing Mount Kenya*§
ASARE KONADU
40 *A Woman in her Prime*
55 *Ordained by the Oracle*
AHMADOU KOUROUMA
239 *The Suns of Independence*
MAZISI KUNENE
211 *Emperor Shaka the Great*†
234 *Anthem of the Decades*†
235 *The Ancestors*†
ALEX LA GUMA
35 *A Walk in the Night**
110 *In the Fog of the Seasons' End*
152 *The Stone Country*
212 *Time of the Butcherbird*
DORIS LESSING
131 *The Grass is Singing*
HUGH LEWIN
251 *Bandiet*
TABAN LO LIYONG
69 *Fixions**
74 *Eating Chiefs**
90 *Frantz Fanon's Uneven Ribs*†
116 *Another Nigger Dead*†
BONNIE LUBEGA
105 *The Outcasts*
YULISA AMADU MADDY
89 *Obasai*‡
137 *No Past, No Present, No Future*

NAGUIB MAHFOUZ
151 *Midaq Alley*
197 *Miramar*
225 *Children of Gebelawi*

NELSON MANDELA
123 *No Easy Walk to Freedom*§

JACK MAPANJE
236 *Of Chameleons and Gods*†

RENE MARAN
135 *Batouala*

DAMBUDZO MARECHERA
207 *The House of Hunger*•
237 *Black Sunlight*

ALI A. MAZRUI
97 *The Trial of Christopher Okigbo*

TOM MBOYA
81 *The Challenge of Nationhood (Speeches)*§

S. O. MEZU
113 *Behind the Rising Sun*

THOMAS MOFOLO
229 *Chaka*

HAM MUKASA
133 *Sir Apolo Kagwa Discovers Britain*§

DOMINIC MULAISHO
98 *The Tongue of the Dumb*
204 *The Smoke that Thunders*

CHARLES L. MUNGOSHI
170 *Waiting for the Rain*

JOHN MUNONYE
21 *The Only Son*
45 *Obi*
94 *Oil Man of Obange*
153 *A Dancer of Fortune*
195 *Bridge to a Wedding*

MARTHA MVUNGI
159 *Three Solid Stones*•

MEJA MWANGI
143 *Kill Me Quick*
145 *Carcase for Hounds*
176 *Going Down River Road*

GEORGE SIMEON MWASE
160 *Strike a Blow and Die*§

JOHN NAGENDA
262 *The Seasons of Thomas Tebo*

NGUGI WA THIONG'O
7 *Weep Not, Child*
17 *The River Between*
36 *A Grain of Wheat*
51 *The Black Hermit*‡
150 *Secret Lives*•
188 *Petals of Blood*
200 *Devil on the Cross*
240 *Detained*§

NGUGI & MICERE MUGO
191 *The Trial of Dedan Kimathi*‡

NGUGI & NGUGI WA MIRII
246 *I Will Marry When I Want*‡

REBEKA NJAU
203 *Ripples in the Pool*

ARTHUR NORTJE
141 *Dead Roots*†

NKEM NWANKWO
67 *Danda*
173 *My Mercedes is Bigger Than Yours*

FLORA NWAPA
26 *Efuru*
56 *Idu*

S. NYAMFUKUDZA
233 *The Non-Believer's Journey*

ONUORA NZEKWU
85 *Wand of Noble Wood*
91 *Blade Among the Boys*

OLUSEGUN OBASANJO
249 *My Command*§

OGINGA ODINGA
38 *Not Yet Uhuru*§

GABRIEL OKARA
68 *The Voice*
183 *The Fisherman's Invocation*†

CHRISTOPHER OKIGBO
62 *Labyrinths*†

KOLE OMOTOSO
102 *The Edifice*
122 *The Combat*

SEMBENE OUSMANE
63 *God's Bits of Wood*
92 *The Money-Order*
175 *Xala*
250 *The Last of the Empire*

YAMBO OUOLOGUEM
99 *Bound to Violence*

MARTIN OWUSU
138 *The Sudden Return*‡

FERDINAND OYONO
29 *Houseboy*
39 *The Old Man and the Medal*

PETER K. PALANGYO
53 *Dying in the Sun*

SOL T. PLAATJE
201 *Mhudi*

R. L. PETENI
178 *Hill of Fools*

LENRIE PETERS
22 *The Second Round*
37 *Satellites*†
238 *Selected Poetry*†

MOLEFE PHETO
258 *And Night Fell*§

J.-J. RABEARIVELO
167 *Translations from the Night*†

MUKOTANI RUGYENDO
187 *The Barbed Wire*

MWANGI RUHENI
139 *The Future Leaders*
156 *The Minister's Daughter*

TAYEB SALIH
47 *The Wedding of Zein*•
66 *Season of Migration to the North*

STANLAKE SAMKANGE
33 *On Trial for my Country*
169 *The Mourned One*
190 *Year of the Uprising*

WILLIAMS SASSINE
199 *Wirriyamu*

KOBINA SEKYI
136 *The Blinkards*‡

SAHLE SELLASSIE
52 *The Afersata*
163 *Warrior King*

FRANCIS SELORMEY
27 *The Narrow Path*

L. S. SENGHOR
71 *Nocturnes*†
180 *Prose and Poetry*

MONGANE SEROTE
263 *To Every Birth Its Blood*

ROBERT SERUMAGA
54 *Return to the Shadows*

WOLE SOYINKA
76 *The Interpreters*

TCHICAYA U TAM'SI
72 *Selected Poems*†

CAN THEMBA
104 *The Will to Die*•

REMS NNA UMEASIEGBU
61 *The Way We Lived*•

LAWRENCE VAMBE
112 *An Ill-Fated People*§

J. L. VIEIRA
202 *The Real Life of Domingos Xavier*
222 *Luuanda*

JOHN YA-OTTO
244 *Battlefront Namibia*§

ASIEDU YIRENKYI
216 *Kivuli and Other Plays*‡

D. M. ZWELONKE
128 *Robben Island*

COLLECTIONS OF PROSE
9 *Modern African Prose*
14 *Quartet*
23 *The Origin of Life and Death*
48 *Not Even God is Ripe Enough*
58 *Political Spider*
73 *North African Writing*
75 *Myths and Legends of the Swahili*
83 *Myths and Legends of the Congo*
109 *Onitsha Market Literature*
118 *Amadu's Bundle*
132 *Two Centuries of African English*
192 *Egyptian Short Stories*
243 *Africa South Contemporary Writings*
254 *Stories from Central and Southern Africa*
256 *Unwinding Threads*
259 *This is the Time*

ANTHOLOGIES OF POETRY
8 *A Book of African Verse*
42 *Messages: Poems from Ghana*
64 *Seven South African Poets*
93 *A Choice of Flowers*
96 *Poems from East Africa*
106 *French African Verse*
129 *Igbo Traditional Verse*
164 *Black Poets in South Africa*
171 *Poems of Black Africa*
192 *Anthology of Swahili Poetry*
215 *Poems from Angola*
230 *Poets to the People*
257 *New Poetry from Africa*

COLLECTIONS OF PLAYS
28 *Short East African Plays*
34 *Ten One-Act Plays*
78 *Short African Plays*
114 *Five African Plays*
127 *Nine African Plays for Radio*
134 *African Theatre*
165 *African Plays for Playing 1*
179 *African Plays for Playing 2*
224 *South African People's Plays*
232 *Egyptian One-Act Plays*

THE WILL TO DIE

Can Themba

selected by Donald Stuart
and Roy Holland

HEINEMANN
London Ibadan Nairobi

Heinemann Educational Books
22 Bedford Square, London WC1B 3HH
P.M.B. *5205 Ibadan* · P.O. Box *45314 Nairobi*
EDINBURGH MELBOURNE AUCKLAND
HONG KONG SINGAPORE KUALA LUMPUR
NEW DELHI KINGSTON PORT OF SPAIN

Heinemann Educational Books Inc.
4 Front Street, Exeter, New Hampshire 03833, USA

ISBN *0 435 90104 4*

First published 1972
Reprinted 1976, 1978, 1983

Printed in Great Britain by
Richard Clay (The Chaucer Press) Ltd,
Bungay, Suffolk

CONTENTS

ACKNOWLEDGEMENTS

The obituary of Can Themba by Lewis Nkosi is reproduced by kind permission of the author and Rajat Neogy, editor of *Transition* (it appeared in No. 34). Ezekiel Mphahlele for '*The Urchin*' (Penguin Books Ltd); Ellis Ayiteh Komey and Ezekiel Mphahlele for '*The Dube Train*' (Faber & Faber Ltd); the proprietors of *The Critic* for '*The Urchin*', '*The Suit*' and '*The Boy with the Tennis Racket*'; the proprietor of *Drum* for '*Terror in the Trains*', '*Boozers Beware of Barberton!*', '*Brothers in Christ*', '*Nude Pass Parade*', '*Let the People Drink*', '*Political Offenders Banned to the Bush*', and '*Henry Nxumalo*'; and the proprietors of *Africa South* for '*Requiem for Sophiatown*', and '*The Bottom of the Bottle*'.

OBITUARY

'The son of a bitch had no business to die . . .'
– *Can Themba at a friend's funeral.*

Time, frustration and despair, with their attendant corrosive drugs – alcohol and suicide – are taking a toll on South African writers. Nat Nakasa. Ingrid Jonker. Now Can Themba. They are all surrendering to something infinitely more difficult to describe. Their deaths are not simply natural deaths even when they are technically so; for even though they do not die at the end of a bullet, flattened against some executioner's wall, their anguish is in so many ways related to the anguish of the people of South Africa. For those of them, like Nat Nakasa and Ingrid Jonker, who committed suicide, this is clear enough; but Can Themba's own anguish and despair led to a suicidal kind of living which was bound to destroy his life at a relatively young age.

At any rate, the deaths of our writers are sometimes more dramatic than most deaths but are nonetheless part of the slow undramatic death of many. Nat Nakasa and Can Themba, personal friends and former colleagues, I knew better than most. I lived in the same house with both of them at different times. After they are gone it seems to me now that there was always something strangely sinister and altogether ominous in their form of detachment and the desperate wit they cultivated, in the mocking cynicism of the one and the love of irony of the other. Each in his own way tried to reduce the South African problem into some form of manageable game one plays constantly with authority without winning, but without losing either. In order to survive and in order to conceal the scars, they laughed, clowned, mocked and finally embraced their 'outlaw' condition with all of its surrounding cloud of romantic tragedy and supposable drama. Lively and self-aware, sensitive as writers can be assumed to be, they were forced by a silly and grotesque regime to exist as though they lacked imagination, consciousness and their superb gift of eloquence. That is to say they were forced to look 'dumb' in order to reassure very dumb white citizens whose sense of security was threatened by any 'native' who seemed imaginative enough and talented enough. Nat Nakasa appreciated the irony and got an enormous bang out of acting upon it. Can Themba similarly grew more ironical and colloquial, affecting to beat the system with a mocking cynicism and an extreme cultural '*underworldism*' of the African township. He fused into the English language the township idiom and rejuvenated tired words with an extreme imagery deriving from a life of danger and violence.

For Can Themba the incursion into 'white' Johannesburg was, so to speak, a kind of temporary surfacing from what he has elsewhere described as 'the swarming, cacophonous, strutting, brawling, vibrating life' of the African township – in his case, Sophiatown. Indeed, Can Themba's agony accentuates the razing to the ground of Sophiatown by the government and the disappearance of many of its folk institutions – the extravagant folk heroes and heroines, shebeens and shebeen queens, singers, nice-time girls, now dispersed by government order to the sprawling, camp-like location ghettos farther out of town. Of the destruction of Sophiatown he has written movingly in 'Requiem for Sophiatown'.

Can Themba's most splendid moments of journalism were therefore the celebration of this life, which is not to say he wished for the continuance of slum conditions in order to engender a spurious vitality but because, for Can Themba, the African township represented the strength and the will to survive by ordinary masses of the African people. In its own quiet way the township represented a dogged defiance against official persecution, for in the township the moments of splendour were very splendid indeed, surpassing anything white Johannesburg could offer. It is true that Can Themba's romanticism drove him in the end to admire more and more the ingenious methods of that survival – the illicit shebeens and illicit traffic, the lawlessness, the everyday street drama in which violence was enacted as a supreme test that one was willing to gamble one's life away for one moment of truth. Such moments of intensity and extreme self-awareness in the face of danger are what the white suburb will never know in its dull bourgeois regularity. In this respect he echoed Ernest Hemingway's romanticism of violence.

Nevertheless, irony is a personal stance; in South Africa it is defensive. Irony cannot defeat a brutal and oppressive regime; it can only assist for a while in concealing the pain and the wounds until the anguish is too deep and unbearable to be contained within a perpetual self-contemplating irony. Nat Nakasa finally committed suicide in New York and no testimony yet offered about his conduct in the last days before his death will give us any clue as to the actual spiritual dilemmas, the immensity in which they presented themselves to him, just before he reached the ultimate of his exile – suicide.

Can Themba, on the other hand, had always disguised his own pain behind a devil-may-take-the-hindlegs kind of attitude and a prodigious reliance on alcohol as a drug. His drinking was phenomenal. The only time I've seen Can Themba's nerve nearly snap was when he was in love with a beautiful young English woman at a time when she was about to leave the country. He himself was trapped – and it seemed forever – in the land of apartheid. At that time I had a glimpse into someone's suffering and I don't care to see it again. Nadine Gordimer's novel, *Occasion for Loving*, may or may not be based on that period in Can Themba's life, but it offers a striking parallel.

His death is not such a mystery to me though it seems again one of the most wasteful deaths we've had in these last three years. The South African actor who passed the news on to me said simply: 'His heart just stopped!' His wife was later quoted as saying she would not mourn him because Can Themba and she had made a vow not to mourn each other when either of them died. He was living in Swaziland at the time, just across the border from South Africa. Like many of our writers, he was already banned from publishing or being quoted in any South African newspaper or publication. This in itself must have been a considerable blow to a writer who considered himself the *poet laureate* of the urban township of South Africa or its new vital, literate proletariat.

Somewhat taller than average, slender, with an impish grin which hovered between self-deprecation and the mockery of others, he gave the impression of a nimble delighted observer, always on the look-out for drama, excitement and fun. He was also a fast talker, a very deft, quick thinker with an equal facility for the apt, if outrageous, phrase. His excitement about ideas, his delight in throwing them up himself or sharing the company of those whose primary interest was ideas, showed him to be first and foremost an intellectual in the original sense of that word. For him the pursuit of ideas was not just an abstract humourless activity: it was a form of *play*. Intellectual activity was nothing if not fun, which led some to regard him as flippant, reckless and irresponsible. For though he had studied English and philosophy, he eschewed the turgid, the solemn and the pretentiously weighty language of those who merely wish to sound abstruse. He lent to his thoughts the same vivid imagery, sharp staccato rhythm of the township language of the urban *tsotsi*, because he himself was the supreme intellectual *tsotsi* of them all, always, in the words of the blues singer, 'raising hell in the neighbourhood'. The neighbourhood in which he raised hell was that sombre, fearful community of the intellect so hideously terrorized by the political regime in South Africa.

Yet in scrutinizing, first, Nat Nakasa's writings one finds in it nothing powerful or astonishing; indeed, one is largely disappointed. There are niggling flashes of brilliance but it is all rather of the order of the breakfast-table columnist, deft, witty, ironical, but nothing more; his reading is minimal. But then he was young and might have developed as he matured.

Can Themba's actual achievements are more disappointing because his learning and reading were more substantial and his talent proven; but he chose to confine his brilliance to journalism of an insubstantial kind. It is almost certain that had Can Themba chosen to write a book on South Africa, it would not only have been an interesting and to use an American word 'insightful' book, but it might have revealed a complex and refined talent for verbalizing the African mood. And no doubt, such a book would have been a valuable addition to the literature of South Africa. As it is, we mourn a talent largely misused or neglected; we mourn what might have been. But to have known Themba, to have heard him speak, is to have known a mind both vigorous and informed, shaped by the city as few other minds are in the rest of Africa.

Lewis Nkosi

I

STORIES

CREPUSCULE

The morning township train cruised into Park Station, Johannesburg, and came to a halt in the dark vaults of the subterranean platforms. Already the young of limb, and the lithe and lissom, had leapt off and dashed for the gate that would let them out. But the rest of us had to wade ponderously, in our hundreds, along the thickening platforms that gathered the populations disgorged by Naledi, Emdeni, Dube, Orlando, Pimville, Nancefield, Kliptown, Springs, Benoni, Germiston. Great maws that spewed their workership over Johannesburg.

I was in the press that trudged in the crowd on the platform. Slowly, good-humouredly we were forced, like the substance of a toothpaste tube, through the little corridor and up the escalator that hoisted us through the outlet into the little space of breath and the teeth of pass-demanding South African Police.

But it was with a lilt in my step that I crossed the parquet foyer floor and slipped through the police net, because I knew which cop to pass by: the one who drank with me at Sis Julia's shebeen of an afternoon off. It was with a lilt, because it was spring as I walked out of Park Station into a pointillist morning with the sun slanting from somewhere over George Goch, and in spring the young ladies wear colourful frocks, glaring against the sunlight and flaring in the mischievous breezes. I joyed as I passed into Hoek Street, seeing the white girls coming up King George Street, the sunlight striking through their dresses, articulating the silhouettes beneath to show me leg and form; things blackmen are supposed to know nothing of, and which the law assininely decrees may not even be imagined.

Funny thing this, the law in all its horrificiency prohibits me, and yet in the streets of Johannesburg I feast for free every morning. And, God, if I try hard enough, I may know for real in Hillbrow every night.

There is a law that says (I'm afraid quite a bit of this will seem like *there is a law that says*) well, it says I cannot make love to a white woman. It is law. But stronger still there is a custom – a tradition, it is called here – that shudders at the sheerest notion that any whiteman could contemplate, or any blackman dare, a love affair across the colour line. They do: whitemen *do* meet and fall in love with black women; blackmen do explore 'ivory towers'. But all this is severely 'agin the law'.

There are also African nationalists who profess horror at the thought that any self-respecting blackman could desire any white woman. They say that no African could ever so debase himself as to love a white woman. This is highly cultivated and pious lying in the teeth of daily slavering in town and in cinema. African girls, who are torturing themselves all the time to gain a whiter complexion, straighter hair and corset-contained posteriors, surely know what their men secretly admire.

As for myself, I do not necessarily want to bed a white woman; I merely insist on my right to want her.

Once, I took a white girl to Sophiatown. She was a girl who liked to go with me and did not have the rumoured South African inhibitions. She did not even want the anthropological knowledge of 'how the other South Africans live'. She just wanted to be with me.

She had a car, an ancient Morris. On the way to Sophiatown of those days, you drove along Bree Street, past the Fordsburg Police Station in the Indian area, past Braamfontein railway station, under the bridge away past the cemetery, past Bridgeman Memorial Hospital (known, strangely, for bringing illegitimate Non-European children into the world), up Hurst Hill, past Talitha Home (a place of detention for delinquent Non-European girls), past aggressive Westdene (sore at the proximity of so many Non-white townships around her), and into Sophiatown.

So that night a blackman and a white woman went to Sophiatown. I first took Janet to my auntie's place in Victoria Road, just opposite the bus terminus. It was a sight to glad a cynic's heart to see my aunt shiver before Janet.

'Mama' – in my world all women equivalents of my mother are mother to me – 'Mama, this is my girl. Where is Tata?' This question, not because my uncle might or might not approve, but because I knew he was terribly fond of brandy, and I was just about to organize a little party; he would not forgive me for leaving him out. But he was not there. He had gone to some meeting of *amagosa* – church-stewards, of whom he was the chief.

'Mama, how about a *doek* for Janet.'

The *doek*! God save our gracious *doek*. A *doek* is a colourful piece of cloth that the African woman wears as headgear. It is tied stylistically into various shapes from Accra to Cape Town. I do not know the history of this innocuous piece of cloth. In Afrikaans, the language of those of our white masters who are of Dutch and Huguenot descent, *doek* meant, variously, a table-cloth, a dirty rag, or a symbol of the slave. Perhaps it was later used by African women in contact with European ideas of beauty who realized that 'they had no hair' and subconsciously hid their heads under the *doek*. Whatever else, the *doek* had come to designate the African woman. So that evening when I said, 'Mama, how about a *doek* for Janet', I was proposing to transform her, despite her colour and her deep blue eyes, into an African girl for the while.

Ma dug into her chest and produced a multi-coloured chiffon *doek*. We stood before the wardrobe mirror while my sisters helped to tie Janet's *doek* in the current township style. To my sisters that night I was obviously a hell of a guy.

Then I took Janet to a shebeen in Gibson Street. I was well-known in that particular shebeen, could get my liquor 'on tick' and could get VIP treatment even without the asset of Janet. With Janet, I was a sensation. Shebeens are noisy drinking places and as we approached that shebeen we could hear the blast of loud-mouthed conversation. But when we entered a haunted hush fell upon the house. The shebeen queen rushed two men off their chairs to make places for us, and: 'What would you have, Mr Themba?'

There are certain names that do not go with Mister, I don't have a clue why. But, for sure, you cannot imagine a Mr Charlie Chaplin or a Mr William Shakespeare or a Mr Jesus Christ. My name – Can Themba – operates in that sort of class. So you can see the kind of sensation we caused, when the shebeen queen addressed me as Mr Themba.

I said, casually as you like, 'A half-a-jack for start, and I suppose you'd like a beer, too, my dear?'

The other patrons of the shebeen were coming up for air, one by one, and I could see that they were wondering about Janet. Some thought that she was Coloured, a South African Mulatto. One said she was white, appending, 'These journalist boys get the best girls.' But it was clear that the *doek* flummoxed them. Even iron-Coloureds, whose stubborn physical appearances veer strongly to the Negroid parent, are proud enough of whatever hair they have to expose it. But this girl wore a *doek*!

Then Janet spoke to me in that tinkling English voice of hers, and I spoke to her, easily, without inhibition, without madamizing her. One chap, who could contain himself no longer, rose to shake my hand. He said, in the argot of the townships, 'Brer Can, you've beaten caustic soda. Look, man, get me fish-meat like this, and s'true's God, I'll buy you a *vung* (a car)!' That sort of thawed the house and everybody broke into raucous laughter.

Later, I collected a bottle of brandy and some ginger ale, and took Janet to my room in Gold Street. There were a few friends and their girls: Kaffertjie (Little Kaffir – he was quite defiantly proud of this name) and Hilda, Jazzboy and Pule, Jimmy, Rockefeller and a Coloured girl we called Madame Defarge because, day or night, she always had clicking knitting needles with her. We drank, joked, conversed, sang and horse-played. It was a night of the Sophiatown of my time, before the government destroyed it.

It was the best of times, it was the worst of times; it was the age of wisdom, it was the age of foolishness; it was the season of Light, it was the season of Darkness; it was the spring of hope, it was the winter of despair; we had everything before us, we had nothing before us; we were all going direct to Heaven, we were all going direct the other way – in short, the period was so far like the present period, that some of its noisiest authorities insisted on its being received, for good or for evil, in the superlative degree of comparison only.

Sometimes I think, for his sense of contrast and his sharp awareness of the pungent flavours of life, only Charles Dickens – or, perhaps, Victor Hugo – could have understood Sophiatown. The government has razed Sophiatown to the ground, rebuilt it, and resettled it with whites. And with appropriate cheek, they have called it Triomf.

That night I went to bed with Janet, chocolate upon cream. I do not know what happened to me in my sleep; the Africans say *amadhlozi* talked to me – the spirits of my forefathers that are supposed to guide my reckless way through this cruel life intervened for once. In the mid of the night, I got up, shook Janet and told her we got to go.

'Ah, Can, you're disturbing me, I want to sleep.'

'Come-ahn, get up!'

'Please, Can, I want to sleep.'

I pulled off the blankets and marvelled awhile at the golden hair that billowed over her shoulders. Then she rose and dressed drowsily.

We got into her ancient Morris and drove to town. I think it was the remembrance of a half-bottle of brandy in her room in Hillbrow that woke me and made me rouse her, more than the timely intervention of the *amadhlozi*. We saw a big, green *Kwela-Kwela* wire-netted lorry-van full of be-batonned white cops driving up Gold Street, but we thought little of it, for the cops, like fleas in our blankets, are always with us. So we spluttered up Hurst Hill into town.

Later, I heard what had happened.

I used to have a young Xhosa girl called Baby. She was not really my class, but in those days for what we called love we Sophiatonians took the high, the middle and the low.

Baby was pathologically fond of parties, the type of parties to which *tsotsis* go. They organize themselves into a club of about half-a-dozen members. On pay-day they each contribute, say £5, and give it to the member whose turn it is. He then throws a party to entertain all the members and their girl-friends. Almost invariably guys trespass on other guys' girls and fights break out. Baby liked this kind of party, but it soon became clear to me that I was risking the swift knife in the dark so long as I associated with her. So I talked it over with her, told her that we should call it a day and that I did not want to clash with her *tsotsi* boyfriends. She readily accepted, saying, 'That-so it is, after all you're a teacher type and you don't suit me.'

So far as I was concerned that had been that.

But that star-crossed night, Baby heard that I was involved with a white girl. She went berserk. I gathered that she went running down Gold Street tearing out her hair and shrieking. At the corner of Gold Street and Victoria Road, she met a group of *tsotsis* playing street football under the street lamp with a tennis ball. They asked her, 'Baby, whassamatter?' She screamed, 'It's Can, he's with a white woman,' and they replied, 'Report him!'

Africans are not on the side of the cops if they can help it. You do not go to a policeman for help or protection or the which way to go. You eschew them. To report a felon to them, good heavens! it is just not done. So for a *tsotsi* to say about anyone, 'Report him!' means the matter is serious.

Baby went to Newlands Police Station and shouted, 'Baas, they're there. They're in bed, my boyfriend and a white woman.' The sergeant behind the counter told her to take it easy, to wait until the criminals were so well-asleep that they might be caught *flagrante delicto*. But Baby was dancing with impatience at 'the law's delay'.

Still, that sergeant wanted to make a proper job of it. He organized a lorry-full of white cops, white cops only, with batons and the right sadistic mental orientation. Or, perhaps, too many such excursions had misadventured before where black cops were suspected of having tipped off their brethren.

When we went down Gold Street, it was them we saw in the green lorry-van bent on a date with a kaffir who had the infernal impertinence to reach over the fence at forbidden fruit.

I understand they kicked open the door of my room and

stormed in, only to find that the birds had flown. One white cop is reported to have said, wistfully, 'Look, man, there are two dents in the pillow and I can still smell her perfume.' Another actually found a long thread of golden hair.

I met Baby a few days later and asked her resignedly, 'But you said we're no more in love, why the big jealous act?'

She replied, 'Even if we've split, you can't shame me for a white bitch.'

I countered, 'But if you still loved me enough to feel jealous, didn't you consider that you were sending me to six months in jail! Baby, it could be seven years, you know.'

'I don't care,' she said. 'But not with a white bitch, Can. And who says that I still love you? It's just that you can't humiliate me with a white bitch.'

I threw up my hands in despair and thought that one of these days I really must slaughter a spotlessly white goat as a sacrifice to the spirits of my forefathers. I have been neglecting my superstitions too dangerously long.

Funny, one of the things seldom said for superstitious belief is that it is a tremendous psychological peg to hang on to. God knows, the vehement attacks made upon the unreason and stark cruelty of superstition and witchcraft practices are warranted. Abler minds than mine have argued this. But I do want to say that those of us who have been detribalized and caught in the characterless world of belonging nowhere, have a bitter sense of loss. The culture that we have shed may not be particularly valuable in a content sense, but it was something that the psyche could attach itself to, and its absence is painfully felt in this whiteman's world where everything significant is forbidden, or 'Not for thee!' Not only the refusal to let us enter so many fields of human experience, but the sheer negation that our spirits should ever assume to themselves identity. Crushing.

It is a crepuscular, shadow-life in which we wander as spectres seeking meaning for ourselves. And even the local, little legalities we invent are frowned upon. The whole atmosphere is charged with the whiteman's general disapproval, and where he does not have a law for it, he certainly has a grimace that cows you. This is the burden of the whiteman's crime against my personality that negatives all the brilliance of intellect and the genuine funds of goodwill so many individuals have. The whole bloody ethos still asphyxiates me. Ingratitude? Exaggeration? Childish, pampered desire for indulgence? Yes-yes, perhaps. But leave us some area in time and experience where we may be true to ourselves. It is so exhausting to have to be in reaction all the time. My race believes in the quick shaft of anger, or of love, or hate, or laughter: the perpetual emotional commitment is foreign to us. Life has contrived so much, such a variegated woof in its texture, that we feel we can tarry only a poignant moment with a little flare of emotion, if we are ever to savour the whole. Thus they call us fickle and disloyal. They have not yet called us hypocritical.

These things I claim for my race, I claim for all men. A little respite, brother, just a little respite from the huge responsibility of being a nice kaffir.

After that adventure in Sophiatown with Janet, I got a lot of sympathy and a lot of advice. I met the boys who had said to Baby, 'Report him!' I was sore because they had singled me out like that and made me the pariah that could be thrown to the wolves. They put their case:

'You see, Brer Can, there's a man here on this corner who plays records of classical music, drinks funny wines and brings whitemen out here for our black girls. Frankly, we don't like it, because these white boys come out here for our girls, but when we meet them in town they treat us like turds. We don't like the way you guys play it with the whites. We're on Baby's side, Brer Can.'

'Look, boys,' I explained, 'You don't understand, you don't understand me. I agree with you that these whites take advantage of our girls and we don't like the way our girls act as if they are special. But all you've done about it is just to sit and sizzle here at them. No-one among you has tried to take revenge. Only I have gone to get a white girl and avenged with her what the whites do to our sisters. I'm not like the guys who procure black girls for their white friends. I seek revenge. I get the white girls – well, it's tough and risky, but you guys, instead of sitting here crying your hearts out, you should get yourselves white girls, too, and hit back.'

I got them, I knew.

One guy said, 'By right, Brer Can's telling the truth.'

Another asked, 'Tell me, Brer Can, how does a white woman taste?'

That was going too far. I had too great a respect for Janet, the *woman*, to discuss that with anybody whether he was white or black.

I said, 'You go find out for yourself.'

The piece of advice I got from the mother of a friend of mine who stayed in the same street, Gold Street, was touching.

She said to me: 'Son, I've heard about your trouble with the white girl. It's you that was foolish. People know that your white girl is around because they recognize the car. If they see it parked flush in front of your house, they say, "Can has got silver-fish". What you should do is to drive the car into my yard here, right to the back of the house so that nobody could see it from the street, and then they wouldn't suspect that you have the white girl in your room down there.'

It seemed to me to be excellent, practical advice.

So the next time I got home with Janet, we drove the car into the yard of my friend's mother, right back behind the house, and walked down in the dead of night to my room.

In the middle of the night, my friend came clattering on the window of my room and shouted, 'Can, get up, the cops!' We got up, got dressed in breathless time, rushed to the car at his mother's place and zoomed out of Sophiatown on a little-used route past St Joseph's Mission through Auckland Park into Hillbrow, where in the heart of the whiteman's flatland we could complete breaking the whiteman's law as, apparently, we could not do in Sophiatown.

Later, I heard the sordid details of what had happened that night. My friend came home late, and overheard his mother and sisters discussing the Morris we had left in their yard. The mother felt that it was not right that I should be messing around with a white woman when she had unmarried daughters of her own and my eligibility rated high. So she sent one of her daughters to go and tell Baby that I was with the white woman again and that I had left the car in their yard. My friend felt that he did not have the time to argue with his family, that his job was to warn us as quickly as he could to get the hell out of there.

As it turned out, I need not have bothered. The darling Afrikaaner at the desk told Baby, 'Look here, woman, every time you have a quarrel with your boyfriend, you rush to us with a cock and bull story. Clear out!'

II

KWASHIORKOR

'Here's another interesting case . . .'

My sister flicked over the pages of the file of one of her case studies, and I wondered what other shipwrecked human being had there been recorded, catalogued, statisticized and analysed. My sister is a social worker with the Social Welfare Department of the Non-European Section of the Municipality of Johannesburg. In other words, she probes into the derelict lives of the unfortunate poor in Johannesburg. She studies their living habits, their recreational habits, their sporting habits, their drinking habits, the incidence of crime, neglect, malnutrition, divorce, aberration, and she records all this in cyclostyled forms that ask the questions ready-made. She has got so good that she could tell without looking whether such-and-such a query falls under paragraph so-and-so. She has got so clinical that no particular case rattles her, for she has met its like before and knows how and where to classify it.

Her only trouble was ferocious Alexandra Township, that hell-hole in Johannesburg where it was never safe for a woman to walk the streets unchaperoned or to go from house to house asking testing questions. This is where I come in. Often I have to escort her on her rounds just so that no township rough-neck molests her. We arranged it lovely so that she only went to Alexandra on Saturday afternoons when I was half-day-off and could tag along.

'Dave,' she said, 'here's another interesting case. I'm sure you would love to hear about it. It's Alex again. I'm interested in the psychological motivations and the statistical significance, but I think you'll get you a human-interest story. I know you can't be objective, but do, I beg you, do take it all quietly and don't mess me up with your sentimental reactions. We'll meet at two o'clock on Saturday, okay?'

That is how we went to that battered house in 3rd Avenue, Alexandra. It was just a lot of wood and tin knocked together gawkily to make four rooms. The house stood precariously a few yards from the sour, cider-tasting gutter, and in the back there was a row of out-rooms constructed like a train and let to smaller families or bachelor men and women. This was the main source of income for the Mabiletsa family – mother, daughter and daughter's daughter.

But let me refer to my sister Eileen's records to get my facts straight.

Mother: Mrs Sarah Mabiletsa, age 62, widow, husband Abner Mabiletsa died 1953 in motor-car accident. Sarah does not work. Medical Report says chronic arthritis. Her sole sources of support are rent from out-rooms and working daughter, Maria. Sarah is dually illiterate.

Daughter: Maria Mabiletsa, age 17, Reference Book No. F/V 118/32N1682. Domestic servant. Educational standard: 5. Reads and writes English, Afrikaans, Sepedi. Convictions: 30 days for shoplifting. One illegitimate child unmaintained and of disputed paternity.

Child: Sekgametse Daphne Lorraine Mabiletsa, Maria's child, age 3 years. Father undetermined. Free clinic attendance. Medical Report: Advanced Kwashiorkor.

Other relatives: Sarah's brother, Edgar Mokgomane, serving jail sentence, 15 years, murder and robbery.

Remarks (Eileen's verdict): This family is desperate. Mother: ineffectual care for child. Child: showing malnutrition effects. Overall quantitative and qualitative nutritional deficiency. Maria: good-time girl, seldom at home, spends earnings mostly on self and parties. Recommend urgent welfare aid and/or intervention.

Although Eileen talks about these things clinically, *objectively*, she told me the story and I somehow got the feel of it.

Abner Mabiletsa was one of those people who was not content with life in the reserves in Pietersburg district where he was born and grew up. He did not see where the tribal set-up of chief and *kgotla* – the tribal council – and customs, taboos, superstitions, witchcraft and the lackadaisical dreariness of rotating with the sun from morn till eve, would take the people and would take him. Moreover, the urge to rise and go out to do things, to conquer and become someone, the impatience of the blood, seized him. So he upped and went to Johannesburg, where else? Everybody went there.

First, there were the ordinary problems of adjustment; the tribal boy had to fit himself into the vast, fast-moving, frenetic life in the big city. So many habits, beliefs, customs had to be fractured overnight. So many reactions that were sincere and instinctive were laughed at in the city. A man was continually changing himself, leaping like a flea from contingency to contingency. But Abner made it, though most of the time he did not know who he was, whither he was going. He only knew that this feverish life had to be lived, and identity became so large that a man sounded ridiculous for boasting he was a Mopedi or a Mosuto or a Xhosa or a Zulu – nobody seemed to care. You were just an African *here*, and somewhere *there* was a whiteman: two different types of humans that impinged, now and then – indeed often – but painfully.

Abner made it. He was helped by his home-boys, those who had come before. They showed him the ropes. They found him a job. They accommodated him those first few months until he found a room of his own in Alexandra. They took him to parties, to girls, to dice schools. Ultimately, they showed him where he could learn to drive a car. Soon, soon, he could negotiate all the byways and back-alleys of Johannesburg by himself. He had escapades, fun, riotous living . . . Until one day one of his escapades became pregnant and bore him a daughter. He paid the *lobola* – that hard-dying custom of paying the bride-price – getting some of his friends and home-boys to stand for him *in loco parentis*; he did not even apprise his folk back home in Pietersburg of his marriage; he did it all himself.

But life in Johannesburg was such that he did not find much time to look after his family. He was not exactly the delinquent father, but there was just not the time or the room for a man to become truly family-bound. Then suddenly, crash! He died in a motor-car accident, and his unprovided-for wife had to make do.

His daughter, Maria, grew up in the streets of Alexandra. The spectre of poverty was always looming over her life; and at the age of fourteen she left school to work in the whiteman's kitchens. It helped, at first, to alleviate the grim want, the ever-empty larder, at home. But soon she got caught up in the froth of Johannesburg's titillating nether life. She had a boy-friend who came pretty regularly to sleep in her room at the back of her place of employment; she had other boy-friends in the city, in the townships, with whom she often slept. And of the billions of human seed so recklessly strewn, one was bound some time to strike target.

When her condition became obvious, Maria nominated the boy she liked best, the swankiest, handsomest, most romantic and most moneyed swain in her repertoire. But he was a dangerous *tsotsi*, and when she told him of what he had wrought, he threatened to beat the living spit out of her. She fondly, foolishly persisted; and he assaulted her savagely. The real boy-friend – the one who slept in her room – felt bitter that she had indicated another. Had he not already boasted to his friends that he had 'bumped' her? Now the whole world judged that he had been cuckolded.

Poor Maria tried the somersault and turned to him, but by then he would have none of it. He effectively told the Native Commissioner, 'I am this girl's second opinion. She does not know who is responsible for her condition. There she stands, now too scared to nominate the man she first fancied, so she looks for a scapegoat, me.'

The commissioner had some biting things to say to Maria, and concluded that he could not, in all conscience, find this man guilty of her seduction. As they say, he threw out the case.

So, Sekgametse Daphne Lorraine was born without a father; an event in Alexandra, in Johannesburg, in all the urban areas of our times, that excites no suprise whatsoever.

First, Maria shed all her love – that is, the anguish and pain she suffered, the bitterness, the humiliation, the sense of desolation and collapse of her tinsel world – upon this infant. But people either perish or recover from wounds; even the worst afflictions do not gnaw at you forever. Maria recovered. She went back to her domestic work, leaving the baby with her mother. She would come home every Thursday – Sheila's Day – or the day-off for all the domestics in Johannesburg. She came to her baby, bringing clothing, blankets, pampering little goodies and smothering treacly love.

But she was young still, and the blood burst inside her once she recovered. Johannesburg was outside there calling, calling, first wooingly, alluringly, then more and more stridently, irresistibly. She came home less often, but remorsefully, and would crush the child to her in those brief moments. Even as she hugged the rose, the thorns tore at her. Then suddenly she came home no more....

'It is quite a typical case of recidivism,' Eileen explained scholastically to me on our way to Alexandra. 'You see, there's a moment's panic as a result of the trauma. The reaction varies according to the victim. One way is that for most of our girls there's a stubborn residue of moral up-bringing from home or school or church, sometimes really only from mamma's personality, and mamma probably comes from an older, steadier, more inhibited and tribe-controlled environment . . .' Eileen shrugged helplessly, ' . . . and detribalization, modernization, adaptation, acculturation, call it what you like, has to tear its way into their psychological pattern, brute-like. At first, before the shock, these girls really just float loosely about in the new freedoms, not really willing evil, not consciously flouting the order, but they're nevertheless playing with fire, and there's no-one knows how to tell them no. Their parents themselves are baffled by what the world's come to and there's no invisible reality like tribe, or comprehensible code like custom or taboo, to keep some kind of balance. Meanwhile, the new dispensation – the superior culture, they call it; the diabolical shadow-life, I call it – pounds at them relentlessly. Suddenly, some traumatic event, a jail-sentence, a sudden encounter with brute, bloody death, or a first pregnancy, pulverizes them into what we credulous monitors consider repentance. It's really the startled whimper of a frightened child vaguely remembering that in some remote distance mamma or tribe or school or church has whispered, "Thou shalt not," and the horror that it's too late.

'But,' Eileen almost cursed out the words, 'the superior culture keeps pounding at them, and it's a matter of time before your repentant maiden sings again, "Jo'burg, here I come".'

I was shaken, 'Eileen, you know that much and yet you continue tinkering with statistics!'

She pulled herself together with an effort. But though she spoke confidently, it sounded unconvincing: 'Lad, I'm a social scientist, not a conjuress.'

So we went to that house in 3rd Avenue, off Selbourne Road. A deep gully ran in front of the house but the uneven street did not allow it to function effectively as a drain, and puddles of murky, noisome water and collected waste-matter stood pooled in it, still, thick, appalling, like foul soup that makes you nauseous – as if some malevolent devil bade you gulp it down. On the other side the rotting carcass of a long-dead dog was sending malodorous miasmata from its surface to befoul the air. And on either side the street, moated by these stinking gullies, lived people.

Eileen jumped smartly over the trench and I followed. We walked into the fenceless yard, round to the back of the house, and she knocked. After a moment a wrinkled old lady opened the door. The plough-shares of the years had wobbled across her face; but then again, you thought it could not have been the years alone that had ravaged her so; something else...

'Oh, come in, nurse.' They called everybody 'nurse' who came to their hovels to promise assuagement of their misery.

Although it was bright day outside, you had to get used to the dark inside, and then when your eyes, by slow degrees, adjusted themselves, things seemed to come at you. A big sideboard tilted into view first. Then a huge stove whose one grey arm reached into the ceiling hole obscenely, and near it a double-bed, perched on four large polish tins filled with sand. The bed was sunken in the middle like a crude canoe, and the blankets on it were yellow with age and threadbare with wear. In the middle of the top blanket was a great hole from some past misadventure, and through the hole glowered a crimson eye, the red disc of a piece-patched quilt-like thing.

I stumbled into a wooden table in the centre, and in my retreat hit a kitchen-dresser. Dark-brown cockroaches scrambled for cover.

'Don't be so clumsy,' Eileen hissed, and in the same syntax, as it were, to the old lady, 'Mother Mabiletsa, it's so dark in here. You really must open that window.'

I had not known there was a window there, but Eileen swept a piece of blanket aside and in flushed the light of day.

'How are you, Mother Mabiletsa? How are the legs to-day? Sit down please and tell me how is the baby.'

Mother Mabiletsa groaned into a chair, and I took a bench by the side of the table. Eileen stood a moment holding the old woman in scrutiny. When the old woman did not reply, Eileen lifted her bag and put it on the table.

'Look, I've brought little Sekgametse some skimmed milk. It's very good for babies, you know.'

I turned to look at the old lady and it seemed to me she was past caring about either Grace or Damnation. She was just enveloped in a dreadful murk of weariness.

She pressed down on arthritic knees, rose painfully and limped into another room. I could hear her moving about, heaving with effort though she sounded alone. Then she came in with a bundle in her arms which she put down on the great bed beside Eileen.

'Come and look,' Eileen whispered to me as she unfurled the bundle.

There sat a little monkey on the bed. It was a two to three years' old child. The child did not cry or fidget, but bore an unutterably miserable expression on its face, in its whole bearing. It was as if she was the grandmother writ small; pathetically, wretchedly she looked out upon the world.

'Is it in pain?' I asked in an anxious whisper.

'No, just wasting away.'

'But she looks quite fat.'

To be sure, she did. But it was a ghastly kind of fatness, the fatness of the 'hidden hunger' I was to know. The belly was distended and sagged towards the bed. The legs looked bent convexly and there were light-brown patches on them, and on the chest and back. The complexion of the skin was unnaturally light here and there so that the creature looked piebald. The normally curly hair had a rusty tint and had lost much of its whorl. Much of it had fallen out, leaving islets of skull surfacing.

The child looked aside towards me, and the silent reproach, the quiet, listless, abject despair flowed from the large eyes wave upon wave. Not a peep, not a murmur. The child made no sound of complaint except the struggling breathing.

But those haunted eyes of despair. Despair? I brooded. To despair, you should have had knowledge before. You should have gone through the tart sensations of experience, have felt the first flush of knowledge, the first stabs of hope, have encountered reality and toyed with the shifting, tantalizing promises that shadow-play across life's tapestries, have stretched out, first tentative arms, then wildly grasping hands, and have discovered the disappointment of the evanescence of all things that come from the voids to tickle men's fancies, sharpen men's appetites and rouse their futile aspirations, only to vanish back into the voids. Ultimately you should have looked into the face of death and known the paralysing power of fear.

What of all this, could this little monkey know? And, yet, there it all was in those tragic eyes.

Then I thought, '*So this is kwashiorkor!*' Hitherto, to me, the name had just been another scare-word that had climbed from the dark caves of medical nomenclature to rear its head among decent folk; it had just been another disgusting digit, a clipped statistic that health officials hurled at us reporters, and which we laced our copy with to impress sensation-seeking editors who would fulminate under headlines like KWASHIORKOR AT YOUR DOOR. It had seemed right, then, almost sufficient that we should link it with the other horrors like 'Infant Mortality', 'Living Below the Bread-Line', 'The Apathy of the People' and 'The Cynical Indifference of the Affluent Society to the Problem'.

But here in this groanless, gloomy room, it seemed indecent to shriek banner headlines when the child, itself, was quiet. It spoke no protest, it offered no resistance.

But while I was romanticizing, my sister was explaining to the old lady how to care for and feed the child, how to prepare and use the skim milk, how often to give it Cod Liver Oil, how often to take it out into the air and the sunlight, how often to take it to the clinic.

Her mistressy voice, now urgent and straining, now clucking and scolding, now anxiously explaining, thinking in English, translating to itself first into Sepedi, begging, stressing, arguing, repeating, repeating, repeating – that restless voice tinkled into my consciousness, bringing me back.

The old lady muttered, 'I hear you, child, but how can I buy all these things with the R1·50c that's left over each month, and how can I carry this child to the clinic with my creaking bones?'

I was subdued.

'Well,' said Eileen later to me as we returned to the bus-stop. 'Think you've seen bottomless tragedy? I could give you figures for kwashiorkor in Alexandra alone . . .'

'Please, Eileen, please.'

My life, a reporter's life, is rather full and hectic, and I am so vortically cast about in the whirlpools of Johannesburg that no single thought, no single experience, however profound, can stay with me for long. A week, two weeks, or less, and the picture of the kwashiorkor baby was jarred out of me, or perhaps lost into the limbo where the psyche hides unpleasant dreams.

Every day during that spell, I had to traffic with the ungodly, the wicked, the unfortunate, the adventurous, the desperate, the outcast and the screwy.

One day, I was in E Court waiting for a rather spectacular theft case to come. I had to sit through the normal run of petty cases. I was bored and fishing inside myself for a worthwhile reverie when suddenly I heard: 'Maria Mabiletsa! Maria Mabiletsa!' My presence of mind hurried back.

The prosecutor said, 'This one is charged with receiving stolen goods, Your Worship.'

A whiteman rose and told the court, 'Your Worship, I appear for the accused. I. M. Karotsky, of Mendelsohn and Jacobs, Sansouci House, 235 Bree Street.'

The prosecutor asked for an adjournment as 'other members of the gang are still at large'.

There was a wrangle about bail, but it was refused and the case was adjourned to August 25th.

It jolted me. After my case, I went down to the cells, and there, after sundry buffetings despite the flashing of my Press Card, I managed to see her.

She was sweet; I mean, looked sweet. Of course, now she was a mixture of fear and defiance, but I could see beyond these façades the real simplicity of her.

I do not know how long she had been in the cells, but she was clean and looked groomed. Her hair was stretched back and neatly tied in the ring behind the crown. She had an oval face, eyes intelligent and alive. Her nose stood out with tender nostrils. Her mouth was delicate but now twisted into a bitter scowl, and a slender neck held her head like the stem of a flower. Her skin-colour was chestnut, but like . . . like . . . like the inside of my hand. She had a slight figure with pouts for breasts, slight hips, but buttocks rounded enough to insist she was African.

She wore atop a white blouse with frills, and amidships one of those skirts cut like a kilt, hugging her figure intimately and suddenly relenting to flare out.

But now she was importunate. For her all time was little, and lots had to be said quickly. Before I could talk to her she said, '*Au-boetie*, please, my brother, please, go and tell Lefty I'm arrested. Marshall Square maybe No. 4. Tell him to bail me out. I'm Maria Mabiletsa, but Lefty calls me Marix. Please, *Au-boetie*, please.'

'Easy Maria,' I soothed, 'I know about you. I'm Dave from *The Courier*.'

'*Hô-man*, *Boeta* Dave, man. You we know, man. I read *The Courier*. But, please, *Boeta* Dave, tell Lefty my troubles, my mother's child.'

A cop was hurrying them away. 'Come'n, *phansi*! – down! *Phansi*! – down!'

'Please, *Au-boetie* Dave, don't forget to tell Lefty!'

'Maria,' I shouted as she was being rushed off, 'I've seen Sekgametse, she's well looked after.'

'Oh! –'

'*Phansi* – down!' Bang! The iron gates fell with a clangour.

That night I told Eileen. She stared at me with knitted brows for a long time. Then she said, 'The main thing is not to panic the old lady. Saturday, you and I will have to go there, but don't do or say anything to make her panic. Leave me to do all the talking.' But I could see Eileen was near panic herself.

Then I went to see Lefty. He was suave, unperturbed, taking all this philosophically.

'You reporter-boys take everything to head. Relax. You must have rhythm and timing. I've already got Karotsky to look after her and tomorrow Marix will be out. Relax, and have a drink.'

She was not out that tomorrow nor the day after. She had to wait for August 25. Meantime, Saturday came and Eileen and I went to the house in 3rd Avenue, Alexandra. When we got there we found – as they say – 'House To Let'. The old lady had heard about what had happened to Maria; she was faced with debts and the threat of starvation, so she packed her things, took the child, and returned to the reserve in Pietersburg.

The neighbours shrugged their shoulders and said, 'What could the old lady do?'

Eileen was livid.

'Dave, do you know what this means?' she erupted. 'It means that child is doomed. In the country, they love children, they look after them, they bring them up according to a code and according to what they *know*, but what they know about the nutrition of children is homicidal and, s'true's God, they live under such conditions of poverty that they may turn cannibals any moment. That's where goes the child I tried to rehabilitate. And when adversity strikes them, when drought comes and the land yields less and less, and the cows' udders dry up, who are the first to go without? The children, those who need the milk most, those who need the proteins, the fats, the oils, the vegetables, the fruit; of the little there is, those who need it most will be the first to go without. There, indeed, they live on mielie-pap and despair. A doctor once told me, Dave, "Kwashiorkor hits hardest between the ages of one and five when protein is needed most and when it's least available to African children." Least available! Why, Dave, why? Because the ignorant African does not realize that when milk is short, give the children first; when meat is little, give the children first. It's not as if . . .' she wailed '. . . it's not as if my over-detribalized self wants to give grown-ups' food to children, but my Sekgametse's sick. I've been trying to coax her back from unnecessary and stupid child-death. Now this.'

Tactlessly, I said, 'Come now, Eileen, you've done your bit. Go and make your report, you're not a nurse, and in any case you can't solve the whole world's troubles one-out.'

'The whole world's troubles!' She spat at me as if I was a child-stealer. 'I only wanted to save that one child, damn you!'

Of course, she made her social worker's report, and other human problems seized her, and I often wondered later whether she had forgotten her kwashiorkor baby. Once, when I asked her if she had heard anything about the baby, she gave a barbed-wire reply, 'Outside our jurisdiction.' It sounded too official to be like Eileen, but I sensed that she felt too raw about it to be anything else than professional, and I held my war within me.

Then I met Maria. It was at a party in Dube, one of those class affairs where thugs and tarts appear in formal dress, and though none of the chicken flew, the liquor flowed.

'Remember me?' I asked her in the provocative style in vogue. She screwed her face and wrinkled her nose and said, 'Don't tell me, don't tell me, I know I know you.' But strain as hard as she tried, she could not identify me. So in mercy I told her I was the news reporter she once sent to Lefty when she was arrested. It half-registered. I told her my sister was the 'nurse' who looked after her Sekgametse. A cloud crossed her brow.

'*Hê*, man, *Au-boetie*, man, Africans are cruel,' she moaned. 'You know, I sent my child to the reserve in Pietersburg, and every month I used to send her nice things until she was the smartest kid in the countryside. Then they bewitched her. *Kaffir-poison!*' she said darkly. 'The child's stomach swelled and swelled with the beast they'd planted in it, until the child died. The Lord God will see those people, *mmcwi*!'

Viciously, I asked: 'And did you ever send the child Soya beans?'

THE URCHIN

One sling of the braces would not keep up on the shoulder, just like one worm of pale-green mucus kept crawling down the chestnut lip and would suddenly dart back like a timid creature. But Macala wore his long pants (surely someone's – someone older's – castaway three-quarter jeans) with a defiant pride just ready to assault the rest of the known world. Other boys his ten-year age only had short pants.

He looked up and down from Mafuta's Chinaman store along Victoria Road, Sophiatown, and he thought of how his day ought to begin. Mafuta's was no good: he kept two too-ferocious dogs in his shop, and fairly-authenticated rumour had it that he also kept a gun that made a terrible noise. But the vistas up and down Victoria Road offered infinite possibilities for a man. To the left, there were queues on queues of half-frightened, half-foolish people who simply asked to be teased. Then Moosa's store with all those fruity, sweety things in the window; but they said Moosa trained at night with irons. Opposite, across Millar Street, there was a Chink butcher, but his counter was fenced off with wire, and Ooh! those cruel knives and hatchets. There must be a lot of money there for it to be protected so formidably. And, next to the butcher, the Bicycle Shop with its blaring juke-box: *Too roo roo roo tu! Too roo roo roo tu-tu!*, where a passer-by girl would suddenly break into a dance step, seductive beyond her years.

All like that, up to Chang's, and from there just the denuded places the demolition squad had left in Sophiatown.

To the right, Macala stared at Benghali House. The only double-storey building in the whole of Sophiatown. In front of it all sorts of pedlars met: sweet-potato sellers, maize sellers, and sweet-reed sellers, African pimpled squash sellers, shoe-lace sellers – all bedamned whether or not the shopkeeper alone held a licence to sell anything.

Macala's eyes glittered as he saw the Ma-Ndebele women squatting in their timeless patience behind their huge dishes of maize-cobs, dried *morogo* peanut cubes, wild fruits like *marula*, *mahlatswa* – things the urban African never sees on trees these days.

To Macala, these women with their quaint and beaded necks, and legs made to look like colourful pythons, were the fairest game.

He stepped off the veranda of Mafuta's shop, off the pavement, and sauntered swaggeringly towards those placid women in front of Benghali House. He was well aware that the street-corner loungers, enormous liars all of them, were watching him, thinking that the slightest move Macala made promised excitement and trouble.

He stopped in front of a Ndebele woman transfixed to her white dish, as if one with it, as if trade meant just being there at the strategic place and time: no bawling, no bartering, no bargaining.

'Dis – how much?' and that to Macala was English with a vengeance. She looked up at him with large baffled eyes, but before she spoke, Macala lifted his foot and trod on the edge of the dish, sending its contents churning out of it into the dust of Victoria Road's pavement. He shrieked with delight as he ran off.

What she hurled at him in virulent Ndebele may have been curses, prayers, lamentations, but to Macala it was reward enough; the kind of thing that proves the superiority of the townsman to these odd creatures from the country. And the passing generation's men and women shook their heads and muttered gloomily, 'the children of today, the children of today...'

His momentum took him to the vegetable vendor just opposite Mafuta's. In fluid career, he seized the handle of the cart and whirled it round and up for the devil of it. Potatoes, onions, pumpkins, cabbages went swirling into the air and plump tomatoes squashed on the macadam. The khaki-coated vendor stood aghast for a second before he broke into imprecations that shuddered even the sordid Sophiatown atmosphere. But Macala was off on his mischievous way.

He had passed the 'Fish and Chips' too fast for another tilt, and met his pals on the corner of Tucker and Victoria: Dipapang, Jungle and Boy-Boy. Together, they should have been 'Our Gang' but their organization was not tight enough for that.

Boy-Boy's was the brain that germinated most of the junior devilry of the team, but he did not quite have Macala's impetuous courage of execution. He looked like a social worker's explanation of 'conditions in the slums': thin to malnourished, delinquent, undisciplined, dedicated to a future gallows. Yet his father was an important man and his mother a teacher. Jungle qualified by the ease with which he could talk of using a knife, in real big-*tsotsi* fashion. Dipapang initiated nothing, thought nothing, was nothing, but was always so willing to join in, trying to finish anything the others cared to start.

'Heit, Macacix!' called Boy-Boy. 'It's how there?'

Macala suddenly felt in the mood for the jargon of the townships. The near-animal, amorphous, quick-shifting lingo that alarms farm-boys and drives cops to all branches of suspicion. But it marks the city slicker who can cope with all its vagaries.

'It's couvert under the corzet,' Macala replied, bobbing his head this way and that to the rhythm.

'Hai, man, bigshot, you must be the reely-reely outlaw in this town,' Boy-Boy parried and lunged.

'Naw,' Macala feinted, 'dis town, Softtown's too small for me. I'll take Western and Corrie and Maclera and London, and smash them into a mashed potato.'

Boy-Boy fell for it, 'Whew!' he whistled, 'don't say you'll crowd me out!'

Macala took him by the throat and went in for the kill, 'Didn't I tell you, buster, to keep out of my country, or else . . .'

He proceeded to carry out the menacing 'or else' by choking Boy-Boy and slowly tripping him over a leg he had slipped behind him until they rolled over as Boy-Boy fell, and tumbled into the gutter.

Boy-Boy gasped, 'Ah give up, boss, da country's yours.'

The mock battle was over and everybody laughed . . . except Jungle. He was reputed to be 'serious' and that meant of the homicidal type. He sat there on the pavement drain with his mournful face, sharpening gratingly on the concrete his 3-Star jack-knife which from some hazy movie memory he called his 'gurkha'. As the laughter trailed off, he suddenly drawled, 'Have you guys heard that Mpedi was arrested yesterday?'

They stared at him in genuine stupefaction. Then Boy-Boy said, 'Yerrrr! How'd it happen, Jungle?'

But Jungle was not one for elaborating a story. Very unsatisfactorily, he said, 'Waal, he was drinking at de English Lady's joint . . . and . . . and dey got him.'

'You mean he didn't shoot it out? You mean dey took him just like dat? But I bet ya dey couldn't put handcuffs on Mpedi!' But Macala was very unhappy about the tame way the idol of the township was arrested.

It was Boy-Boy who made a story of it. 'Yerrr! But *there* is an outee – a great outlaw!' He rose from the pavement and stood before the fascinated gaze of his pals. He stuck his thumbs into his belt and swayed his hips as he strutted up and down before them. Then he mimicked the bull-brained fearlessness of Mpedi, the mirror and form of almost all young Sophiatown, the clattering terror of men, and the perennial exasperation of the police station across the road.

'Ya! Da room was full – full to da door. Clevers, bigshots, boozers, bamboos, coat-hangers, hole-diggers, and bullets, blondes, figure 8's and capital I's, wash-planks and two-ton trucks. Da boys were in de stack and da dames were game . . .

'Then Bura Mpedi stepped in, his eyes blood-red. The house went dead-still. Ag, man, Bura Mpedi, man. He stood there and looked left . . . and looked right . . . His man was not there. He stepped in some more. The house was dead. He grabbed a beer from the nearest table and slugged it from the bottle. Who would talk?' Boy-Boy's upper lip curled up on one side in utter contempt, 'Heh, who would talk!'

Macala and his pals were caught in Boy-Boy's electric pause. Even Jungle was aroused by this dramatic display of township bullycraft.

Boy-Boy's histrionics continued, 'Yerrrre! A drunk girl came from under a table, and tried Mpedi for a drink. "Au, Bura Mpedi, give me a beer." Bura Mpedi put a boot on her shoulder and pushed her back under da table. Hai, man, hai man, dat outee is coward-cool, man. And he hates cherry coat-hangers. But dat night his eyes were going all over looking for Mahlalela. Yeffies! If he'd caught Mahlalela dat night . . . !'

Lifted by the wide-eyed admiration of his pals, Boy-Boy went on to surpass himself. He flung out his right arm recklessly, and declared, 'Bat dat's nutting yet! You should have seen Bura Mpedi when dey sent four lean cops to come and take him. Payroll robbery, Booysens . . . one thousand pound! Assault with Grievous Bodily Harm, Newlands . . . three men down and out! Housebreakin' 'n *Thatha* . . . Lower Houghton!

'Dey came, man dey came. Four cops; two had guns, two had small inches. Dey surrounded da joint in Gibson Street, and dey called out to him to give up. Dey didn't know Mpedi with moonwash in his brains and a human intestine round his waist. He drew his point-three-five and his forty-five, and he came out shooting: Twah! Rwah! Rwah! Da two cops with the small inches ducked into a shebeen near by and ordered themselves a ha' nip brandy. One with da gun ran down Gibson Street for reinforces. Da last cop took a corner and decided to shoot it out with Mpedi. But da bullets came so fast he never got a chance to poke out a shot.

'Hee-e-e, I tell you Mpedi was da outee.' Then, still carried forward by the vibrance of his enthusiasm, Boy-Boy rounded off his dramatization by backing away slowly as he fired off imaginary guns, and barked, 'Twah! Twah! Twah!'

But the elation that had swelled up in Macala was now shot through with envy. 'How come,' he grumbled, 'Da cops got him so easy now?' Yet what really worried him was that he knew how far he was beneath the fabulous Mpedi; that even in his own weight division, he could not make such an awe-inspiring impression. He was not even as good an actor as Boy-Boy to recount and represent the exploits of the almighties. He looked at Boy-Boy bitterly and told himself, 'I'll beat his brains out if he gets smart with me.'

It was Jungle who wrenched him out of his sour reverie. 'Boys, I think we should go finish off da Berliners,' Jungle said, prosaically.

A flash of fear leapt into Boy-Boy's eyes, for he knew this meant war. Macala was himself a bit scared, but seeing the fear in Boy-Boy, he screwed his heart through a hole too small for it.

And Jungle's 'gurkha' went on scraping the pavement concrete, *screech-screech! screech-screech!*

'Come-ahn, let's go,' Macala suddenly decided.

They swaggered along Victoria Road, filling it from pavement to pavement as if they were a posse. Silent. Full of purpose. Deliberately grim. Boys and girls scampered for cover. Grownups stepped discreetly out of their way. Only the bigger tsotsis watched them with pride, and shouted encouragements like '*Da men who rule da town! Tomorrow's outees!*'

On the corner of Meyer Street, they broke up a ring of young dicers and forced them to join up. Along the way they collected non-schoolgoing loafers who lounged against shop walls; blue-jeaned youngsters who twisted the arms of school-girls in rough love; odd-job boys who ran errands for shopkeepers; truants, pickpockets, little thugs, within their age limit – the lot.

By the time they turned into Edith Street, they were a miniature army of hell-bent ruffians. Macala led them and felt the strange thrill of the force behind him. He chose Edith Street because it rose into a rocky hill with plenty of stones for ammunition, and dropped suddenly into that part of Sophiatown they called *Berlin*, where the walls were smeared with crude swastikas.

Macala split his men into two groups. Those with thick, bronze buckle belts were to go under Jungle through a cut in the row of houses precariously perched on huge boulders.

The excitement chopped Macala's breath into collops as he gave out his instructions. 'You boys get dem from de back. You start de war. When dey come running up Edward Road, dey'll meet us. Use dat butcher of yours Uncle Jungle.'

Jungle gave one of his rare smiles, and his men took position.

Macala and his group, first placing a sentinel on the hill-top, slowly clambered down the rocks and waited for Jungle to get around.

Though going into the den of the enemy, Jungle did not find it difficult to rout them. There was a biggish group of them playing dice in the usual ring, and when he swooped upon them, they instinctively thought it was the police and dashed up Edward Road, sticks and buckle belts raining on their heads.

Jungle himself had chosen a heftily-built fellow and was stabbing at him as he ran. Boy-Boy was later to describe it graphically, 'Yerre! Dat guy just wouldn't fall. Jungle had him – zip! But he ran on. Jungle caught him again in the neck – zip! He stumbled and trotted on his hands and feet. Jungle got him in the buttock – zip! But, yerrr! He just wouldn't fall!'

Before the Berliners could rally and make a stand, they had run into Macala's stone-throwing division. Though very one-sided, the fight became fierce. The Berliners were now fighting, and because they were trapped and because they had to fight with their bare hands most of the time, they became young devils from the playgrounds of Hell.

Stones and all sorts of other missiles were hurled in all directions. Knives were brandished and plunged, big-buckled belts were swung in whistling arcs, arms were flailed in the centre of the imbroglio with desperate savagery. Women screamed, shops closed, traffic diverted itself. Now and then, a blood-bespattered boy would stagger off the street to a side wall just to sit down and watch, too done in to flee.

Then suddenly came the shrill warning cry, '*Arrara! Arrarayii!*' The action stopped almost as abruptly as those ancient films which froze in mid-motion and transfixed the movement into a photograph. And just as suddenly after, they scattered all pell-mell. When the police van came round the corner, it was impossible to decide which flee-ers to pursue. For, now, everybody was running up and down and off the streets. The scores of small boys, ordinary pedestrians who had just alighted upon the scene, Fah-fee runners with full-blown cheeks a-chumping the incriminating tickets of their illicit lottery; everybody was running. In Sophiatown, you do not stop to explain to the police that you had nothing to do with it, or that you knew some of the culprits and could help the police.

The mobile squad were satisfied with merely clearing the street.

Breathless and bruised, Macala found himself at the open commonage called Maccauvlei, adjacent to Waterval Hospital, which served as the waste dumps to the city, and 'golf course' to those Africans who went in for the sport of leisure. Macala knew that most of his gang would sooner or later find their way there. He sat on a mound of ash, gasping heavily.

By the time Boy-Boy had arrived, he had regained his breath, and was pitching chalky, burnt-out pebbles rather pointlessly. Jungle came, for once, apparently, in his seventh heaven. Dipapang, too, grinned happily though his shirt had been torn down and hung like a hula. A few other stragglers from the Black Caps joined them, and then came the News. News that oddly took the shape of 'They say'.

'Dey say,' announced one urchin, 'dat one of de Berliners is dead.'

Stultifying fright seized them all. Some small boy simply broke out crying. Macala had trouble with a choking clod in his throat.

'Dey say,' came in another boy, 'de Berliners are going to call in de Big Berliners.'

'Agh,' grunted Macala in contempt, 'we'll go'n tell Bura Shark.'

'Dey say de cops're going to round us all up tonight.'

Despite all their bravado, all their big-shot stances and their blistering contempt for cops and the law, there is one thing that this knighthood really fears, and it was expressed by a crackling of interjections from each according to his own lights.

'Six lashes and reformatory!'

'De cane and off to a farm!'

'Cuts with a light cane and no fine!'

Someone elaborated the procedure by filling in the gory details: 'Dey say, two huge cops hold you down over a big bench an' you got nothin' on. You can't move. Now, maybe de magistrate he said "Six cuts". Dat's nothin'. If you cry, for every one you get two. An' dose cops who give de lashes, dey train for you, dey pick up weightlifting for you, dey grip a grip all day for you. Den when de other cops got you on de bench, an' you can't move, an' you don't want to cry, de lashing cop he takes de cane, he swishes it over his head, one-two-three, whish! De tattoo jumps up on your buttocks.

'Dey say, he den goes to sit down, lights a sigareete, and talks with de other cops. Den he comes again. One of de cops holding you turns your head so you can see de lashing cop coming. He swishes de cane, one-two-three, whish! 'Nother tattoo comes up, dis time with blood. Red blood from your buttocks. He goes for 'nother puff at his cigarette, or maybe he looks for his tea dis time.

'He comes again. Dis time he sneezes his nose on your buttocks, and makes jokes how black buttocks is tough. He swishes the cane, one-two-three, whish! If you don't cry, maybe you get your six lashes straight. But if you cry, only just *Maye Babo* – oh-ho-ho! . . .

'An' dey say, sometimes after you get lashes, six days, two weeks, you can't sit in de bus, you give your seat to de aunties. Hai, dat cane dey keep in de salt water when nobody get lashes!'

By that time the horror of the prospect had seeped through every delinquent soul. It was Macala who spoke first.

He said determinedly, 'Me, I'm not going home tonight.'

But Boy-Boy did not like the idea. He knew that his mother would not rest until she had found out where he was. Worse still, she might even go ask the police to help her find him. 'Naw, Macacix, I'm going home. I don't like cops catching me when my ma is not there. I'm going home.'

As he walked away, the whole little gang suddenly broke up and walked home their different ways. As they scattered, Macala went frantic with panic. With consternation twisted in his face and his arms floating like a blind man's in front of him, he looked half-comic as he stood on that mount of ash.

'Hey, hey, you guys won't leave me alone. We're de boys . . .'

He heard a sound of impatience behind him, 'Aargh! Let them go, Macala.' He turned round and reeled unsteadily a little as he saw Jungle standing there, not looking frightened at all.

'Wh-what you going to do, Jungle?'

Jungle took out his 'gurkha' and scraped it across his palm from left to right, right to left. Then he said, 'I'm going home, Macala,' and that mournful expression crept across his countenance. 'And when de cops come to get me tonight . . .' He made an ugly motion with his knife under his chin. He walked away with the slow lanky movement of that gawky body of his.

By the time Macala decided to leave Maccauvlei, it was getting dark. But he knew where he was going. Rather unnecessarily, he skulked along the fences of the street, looking this way and that. Now and then, he would petrify at the zoom of a passing car or duck into an alley when headlights bore goldenly through the dark of the street. But ultimately he reached the open space where Gerty, Bertha, and Toby Streets used to be. He saw the dark building for which he was headed. He ran forward and stopped in front of it, but this side of the street. Slowly now. Somewhere here there was a night-watchman, a Zulu with a thick black beard and barbel moustache, black uniform and black face that rubbed him out of sight in the dark, and a gnarled knobkerrie known to have split skulls.

But Macala knew where the corrugated-iron fence had snarled out a lip of entrance for him. He went on his hands and knees, and crawled away from the immense double gate towards this entrance. He found it and coiled himself inside. He knew there were stacks of corrugated iron in this timber yard, and if he touched them, the racket would alert the night-watchman. So he did not go far, just nestled himself near his exit.

A little breeze was playing outside, hasting a piece of paper down the street, and now and then a bus or lorry would thunder by. But Macala slept, occasionally twitching in the hidden mechanics of sleep. Far from where he could hear, a woman's voice was calling stridently, 'Mac-a-a-ala! Mac-a-a-a-la! Hai, that child will one day bring me trouble.'

THE SUIT

Five-thirty in the morning, and the candlewick bedspread frowned as the man under it stirred. He did not like to wake his wife lying by his side – as yet – so he crawled up and out by careful peristalsis. But before he tiptoed out of his room with shoes and socks under his arm, he leaned over and peered at the sleeping serenity of his wife: to him a daily matutinal miracle.

He grinned and yawned simultaneously, offering his wordless Te Deum to whatever gods for the goodness of life; for the pure beauty of his wife; for the strength surging through his willing body; for the even, unperturbed rhythms of his passage through days and months and years – it must be – to heaven.

Then he slipped soundlessly into the kitchen. He flipped aside the curtain of the kitchen window, and saw outside a thin drizzle, the type that can soak one to the skin, and that could go on for days and days. He wondered, head aslant, why the rain in Sophiatown always came in the morning when workers had to creep out of their burrows; and then at how blistering heat-waves came during the day when messengers had to run errands all over; and then at how the rain came back when workers knocked off and had to scurry home.

He smiled at the odd caprice of the heavens, and tossed his head at the naughty incongruity, as if, 'Ai, but the gods!'

From behind the kitchen door, he removed an old rain cape,

peeling off in places, and swung it over his head. He dashed for the lavatory, nearly slipping in a pool of muddy water, but he reached the door. Aw, blast, someone had made it before him. Well, that is the toll of staying in a yard where twenty . . . thirty other people have to share the same lean-to. He was dancing and burning in that climactic moment when trouser-fly will not come wide soon enough. He stepped round the lavatory and watched the streamlets of rainwater quickly wash away the jet of tension that spouted from him. That infinite after-relief. Then he dashed back to his kitchen. He grabbed the old baby bath-tub hanging on a nail under the slight shelter of the gutterless roof-edge. He opened a large wooden box and quickly filled the bath-tub with coal. Then he inched his way back to the kitchen door and inside.

He was huh-huh-huhing one of those fugitive tunes that cannot be hidden, but often just occur and linger naggingly in the head. The fire he was making soon licked up cheerfully, in mood with his contentment.

He had a trick for these morning chores. While the fire in the old stove warmed up, the water kettle humming on it, he gathered and laid ready the things he would need for the day: briefcase and the files that go with it; the book that he was reading currently; the letters of his lawyer boss which he usually posted before he reached the office; his wife's and his own dry-cleaning slips for the Sixty-Minutes; his lunch tin solicitously prepared the night before by his attentive wife; and, today, the battered rain cape. By the time the kettle on the stove sang (before it actually boiled), he poured water from it into a wash basin, refilled and replaced it on the stove. Then he washed himself carefully: across the eyes, under, in and out the armpits, down the torso and in between the legs. This ritual was thorough, though no white man a-complaining of the smell of wogs knows anything about it. Then he dressed himself fastidiously. By this time he was ready to prepare breakfast.

Breakfast! How he enjoyed taking in a tray of warm breakfast to his wife, cuddled in bed. To appear there in his supremest immaculacy, tray in hand when his wife comes out of ether to behold him. These things we blacks want to do for our own . . .

not fawningly for the whites for whom we bloody-well got to do it. He felt, he denied, that he was one of those who believed in putting his wife in her place even if she was a good wife. Not he.

Matilda, too, appreciated her husband's kindness, and only put her foot down when he offered to wash up also.

'Off with you,' she scolded him on his way.

At the bus-stop he was a little sorry to see that jovial old Maphikela was in a queue for a bus ahead of him. He would miss Maphikela's raucous laughter and uninhibited, bawdy conversations in fortissimo. Maphikela hailed him nevertheless. He thought he noticed hesitation in the old man, and a slight clouding of his countenance, but the old man shouted back at him, saying that he would wait for him at the terminus in town.

Philemon considered this morning trip to town with garrulous old Maphikela as his daily bulletin. All the township news was generously reported by loud-mouthed heralds, and spiritedly discussed by the bus at large. Of course, 'news' included views on bosses (scurrilous), the Government (rude), Ghana and Russia (idolatrous), America and the West (sympathetically ridiculing), and boxing (bloodthirsty). But it was always stimulating and surprisingly comprehensive for so short a trip. And there was no law of libel.

Maphikela was standing under one of those token bus-stop shelters that never keep out rain nor wind nor sun-heat. Philemon easily located him by his noisy ribbing of some office boys in their khaki-green uniforms. They walked together into town, but from Maphikela's suddenly subdued manner, Philemon gathered that there was something serious coming up. Maybe a loan.

Eventually, Maphikela came out with it.

'Son,' he said sadly, 'if I could've avoided this, believe you me I would, but my wife is nagging the spice out of my life for not talking to you about it.'

It just did not become blustering old Maphikela to sound so grave and Philemon took compassion upon him.

'Go ahead, dad,' he said generously. 'You know you can talk to me about anything.'

The old man gave a pathetic smile. 'We-e-e-ll, it's not really any of our business . . . er . . . but my wife felt . . . you see. Damn it all! I wish these women would not snoop around so much.' Then he rushed it. 'Anyway, it seems there's a young man who's going to visit your wife every morning... ah... for these last bloomin' three months. And that wife of mine swears by her heathen gods you don't know a thing about it.'

It was not quite like the explosion of a devastating bomb. It was more like the critical breakdown in an infinitely delicate piece of mechanism. From outside the machine just seemed to have gone dead. But deep in its innermost recesses, menacing electrical flashes were leaping from coil to coil, and hot, viscous molten metal was creeping upon the fuel tanks...

Philemon heard gears grinding and screaming in his head...

'Dad,' he said hoarsely, 'I... I have to go back home.'

He turned round and did not hear old Maphikela's anxious, 'Steady, son. Steady, son.'

The bus ride home was a torture of numb dread and suffocating despair. Though the bus was now emptier Philemon suffered crushing claustrophobia. There were immense washerwomen whose immense bundles of soiled laundry seemed to baulk and menace him. From those bundles crept miasmata of sweaty intimacies that sent nauseous waves up and down from his viscera. Then the wild swaying of the bus as it negotiated Mayfair Circle hurtled him sickeningly from side to side. Some of the younger women shrieked delightedly to the driver, '*Fuduga!* . . . Stir the pot!' as he swung his steering-wheel this way and that. Normally, the crazy tilting of the bus gave him a prickling exhilaration. But now...

He felt like getting out of there, screamingly, elbowing everything out of his way. He wished this insane trip were over, and then again, he recoiled at the thought of getting home. He made a tremendous resolve to gather in all the torn, tingling threads of his nerves contorting in the raw. By a merciless act of will, he kept them in subjugation as he stepped out of the bus back in the Victoria Road terminus, Sophiatown.

The calm he achieved was tense . . . but he could think now . . . he could take a decision . . .

With almost boyishly innocent urgency, he rushed through his kitchen into his bedroom. In the lightning flash that the eye can whip, he saw it all . . . the man beside his wife . . . the chestnut arm around her neck . . . the ruffled candlewick bedspread . . . the suit across the chair. But he affected not to see.

He opened the wardrobe door, and as he dug into it, he cheerfully spoke to his wife, 'Fancy, Tilly, I forgot to take my pass. I had already reached town, and was going to walk up to the office. If it hadn't been for wonderful old Mr Maphikela.'

A swooshing noise of violent retreat and the clap of his bedroom window stopped him. He came from behind the wardrobe door and looked out from the open window. A man clad only in vest and underpants was running down the street. Slowly, he turned round and contemplated . . . the suit.

Philemon lifted it gingerly under his arm and looked at the stark horror in Matilda's eyes. She was now sitting up in bed. Her mouth twitched, but her throat raised no words.

'Ha,' he said, 'I see we have a visitor,' indicating the blue suit. 'We really must show some of our hospitality. But first, I must phone my boss that I can't come to work today . . . mmmm-er, my wife's not well. Be back in a moment, then we can make arrangements.' He took the suit along.

When he returned he found Matilda weeping on the bed. He dropped the suit beside her, pulled up the chair, turned it round so that its back came in front of him, sat down, brought down his chin on to his folded arms before him, and waited for her.

After a while the convulsions of her shoulders ceased. She saw a smug man with an odd smile and meaningless inscrutability in his eyes. He spoke to her with very little noticeable emotion; if anything, with a flutter of humour.

'We have a visitor, Tilly.' His mouth curved ever so slightly. 'I'd like him to be treated with the greatest of consideration. He will eat every meal with us and share all we have. Since we have no spare room, he'd better sleep in here. But the point is, Tilly that you will meticulously look after him. If he vanishes or anything else happens to him . . .' A shaft of evil shot from his eye . . . 'Matilda, I'll kill you.'

He rose from the chair and looked with incongruous supplication at her. He told her to put the fellow in the wardrobe for the time being. As she passed him to get the suit, he turned to go. She ducked frantically, and he stopped.

'You don't seem to understand me, Matilda. There's to be no violence in this house if you and I can help it. So, just look after that suit.' He went out.

He went out to the Sophiatown Post Office, which is placed on the exact line between Sophiatown and the white man's surly Westdene. He posted his boss's letters, and walked to the beer-hall at the tail end of Western Native Township. He had never been inside it before, but somehow the thunderous din laved his bruised spirit. He stayed there all day.

He returned home for supper . . . and surprise. His dingy little home had been transformed, and the air of stern masculinity it had hitherto contained had been wiped away, to be replaced by anxious feminine touches here and there. There were even gay, colourful curtains swirling in the kitchen window. The old-fashioned coal stove gleamed in its blackness. A clean, chequered oil cloth on the table. Supper ready.

Then she appeared in the doorway of the bedroom. Heavens! here was the woman he had married; the young, fresh, cocoa-coloured maid who had sent rushes of emotion shuddering through him. And the dress she wore brought out all the girlishness of her, hidden so long beneath German print. But no hint of coquettishness, although she stood in the doorway and slid her arm up the jamb, and shyly slanted her head to the other shoulder. She smiled weakly.

'What makes a woman like this experiment with adultery?' he wondered.

Philemon closed his eyes and gripped the seat of his chair on both sides as some overwhelming, undisciplined force sought to catapult him towards her. For a moment some essence glowed fiercely within him, then sank back into itself and died . . .

He sighed and smiled sadly back at her, 'I'm hungry, Tilly.'

The spell snapped, and she was galvanized into action. She prepared his supper with dexterous hands that trembled a little only when they hesitated in mid-air. She took her seat opposite him, regarded him curiously, clasped her hands waiting for his prayer, but in her heart she murmured some other, much more urgent prayer of her own.

'Matilda!' he barked. 'Our visitor!' The sheer savagery with which he cracked at her jerked her up, but only when she saw the brute cruelty in his face did she run out of the room, toppling the chair behind her.

She returned with the suit on a hanger, and stood there quivering like a feather. She looked at him with helpless dismay. The demoniacal rage in his face was evaporating, but his heavy breathing still rocked his thorax above the table, to and fro.

'Put a chair, there.' He indicated with a languid gesture of his arm. She moved like a ghost as she drew a chair to the table.

'Now seat our friend at the table . . . no, no, not like that. Put him in front of the chair, and place him on the seat so that he becomes indeed the third person.'

Philemon went on relentlessly: 'Dish up for him. Generously. I imagine he hasn't had a morsel all day, the poor devil.'

Now, as consciousness and thought seeped back into her, her movements revolved so that always she faced this man who had changed so spectacularly. She started when he rose to open the window and let in some air.

She served the suit. The act was so ridiculous that she carried it out with a bitter sense of humiliation. He came back to sit down and plunge into his meal. No grace was said for the first time in this house. With his mouth full, he indicated by a toss of his head that she should sit down in her place. She did so. Glancing at her plate, the thought occurred to her that someone, after a long famine, was served a sumptuous supper, but as the food reached her mouth it turned to sawdust. Where had she heard it?

Matilda could not eat. She suddenly broke into tears.

Philemon took no notice of her weeping. After supper, he casually gathered the dishes and started washing up. He flung a dry cloth at her without saying a word. She rose and went to stand by his side drying up. But for their wordlessness, they seemed a very devoted couple.

After washing up, he took the suit and turned to her. 'That's how I want it every meal, every day.' Then he walked into the bedroom.

So it was. After that first breakdown, Matilda began to feel that her punishment was not too severe, considering the heinousness of the crime. She tried to put a joke into it, but by slow, unconscious degrees, the strain nibbled at her. Philemon did not harass her much more, so long as the ritual with the confounded suit was conscientiously followed.

Only once, he got one of his malevolent brainwaves. He got it into his head that 'our visitor' needed an outing. Accordingly the suit was taken to the dry-cleaners during the week, and, come Sunday, they had to take it out for a walk. Both Philemon and Matilda dressed for the occasion. Matilda had to carry the suit on its hanger over her back and the three of them strolled leisurely along Ray Street. They passed the church crowd in front of the famous Anglican Mission of Christ the King. Though the worshippers saw nothing unusual in them, Matilda felt, searing through her, red-hot needles of embarrassment, and every needle-point was a public eye piercing into her degradation.

But Philemon walked casually on. He led her down Ray Street and turned into Main Road. He stopped often to look into shop windows or to greet a friend passing by. They went up Toby Street, turned into Edward Road, and back home To Philemon the outing was free of incident, but to Matilda it was one long, excruciating incident.

At home, he grabbed a book on Abnormal Psychology, flung himself into a chair and calmly said to her, 'Give the old chap a rest, will you, Tilly?'

In the bedroom, Matilda said to herself that things could not go on like this. She thought of how she could bring the matter to a head with Philemon; have it out with him once and for all. But the memory of his face, that first day she had forgotten to entertain the suit, stayed her. She thought of running away, but where to? Home? What could she tell her old-fashioned mother had happened between Philemon and her? All right, run away clean then. She thought of many young married girls who were divorcees now, who had won their freedom.

What had happened to Staff Nurse Kakile? The woman drank heavily now, and when she got drunk, the boys of Sophiatown passed her around and called her the Cesspot.

Matilda shuddered.

An idea struck her. There were still decent, married women around Sophiatown. She remembered how after the private schools had been forced to close with the advent of Bantu Education, Father Harringay of the Anglican Mission had organized Cultural Clubs. One, she seemed to remember, was for married women. If only she could lose herself in some cultural activity, find absolution for her conscience in some doing good; that would blur her blasted home life, would restore her self-respect. After all, Philemon had not broadcast her disgrace abroad . . . nobody knew; not one of Sophiatown's slander-mongers suspected how vulnerable she was. She must go and see Mrs Montjane about joining a Cultural Club. She must ask Philemon now if she might . . . she must ask him nicely.

She got up and walked into the other room where Philemon was reading quietly. She dreaded disturbing him, did not know how to begin talking to him . . . they had talked so little for so long. She went and stood in front of him, looking silently upon his deep concentration. Presently, he looked up with a frown on his face.

Then she dared, 'Phil, I'd like to join one of those Cultural Clubs for married women. Would you mind?'

He wrinkled his nose and rubbed it between thumb and index finger as he considered the request. But he had caught the note of anxiety in her voice and thought he knew what it meant.

'Mmmm,' he said, nodding. 'I think that's a good idea. You can't be moping around here all day. Yes, you may, Tilly.' Then he returned to his book.

The Cultural Club idea was wonderful. She found women like herself, with time (if not with tragedy) on their hands, engaged in wholesome, refreshing activities. The atmosphere was cheerful and cathartic. They learned things and they did things. They organized fêtes, bazaars, youth activities, sport, music, self-help and community projects. She got involved in committees, meetings, debates, conferences. It was for her a whole new venture into humancraft, and her personality blossomed. Philemon gave her all the rein she wanted.

Now, abiding by that silly ritual at home seemed a little thing . . . a very little thing . . .

Then one day she decided to organize a little party for her friends and their husbands. Philemon was very decent about it. He said it was all right. He even gave her extra money for it. Of course, she knew nothing of the strain he himself suffered from his mode of castigation.

There was a week of hectic preparation. Philemon stepped out of its cluttering way as best he could. So many things seemed to be taking place simultaneously. New dresses were made. Cakes were baked: three different orders of meat prepared; beef for the uninvited chancers; mutton for the normal guests; turkey and chicken for the inner pith of the club's core. To Philemon, it looked as if Matilda planned to feed the multitude on the Mount with no aid of miracles.

On the Sunday of the party, Philemon saw Matilda's guests. He was surprised by the handsome grace with which she received them. There was a long table with enticing foods and flowers and serviettes. Matilda placed all her guests round the table, and the party was ready to begin in the mock-formal township fashion. Outside a steady rumble of conversation went on where the human odds and ends of every Sophiatown party had their 'share'.

Matilda caught the curious look on Philemon's face. He tried to disguise his edict when he said, 'Er . . . the guest of honour.'

But Matilda took a chance. She begged, 'Just this once, Phil.'

He became livid. 'Matilda!' he shouted, 'Get our visitor!' Then with incisive sarcasm, 'Or are you ashamed of him?'

She went ash-grey; but there was nothing for it but to fetch her albatross. She came back and squeezed a chair into some corner, and placed the suit on it. Then she slowly placed a plate of food before it. For a while the guests were dumbfounded.

Then curiosity flooded in. They talked at the same time. 'What's the idea, Philemon?' . . . 'Why must she serve a suit?' . . . 'What's happening?' Some just giggled in a silly way. Philemon carelessly swung his head towards Matilda. 'You better ask my wife. She knows the fellow best.'

All interest beamed upon poor Matilda. For a moment she could not speak, all enveloped in misery. Then she said, unconvincingly, 'It's just a game that my husband and I play at mealtime.' They roared with laughter. Philemon let her get away with it.

The party went on, and every time Philemon's glare sent Matilda scurrying to serve the suit each course; the guests were no-end amused by the persistent mock-seriousness with which this husband and wife played out their little game. Only, to Matilda, it was no joke; it was a hot poker down her throat. After the party, Philemon went off with one of the guests who had promised to show him a joint 'that sells genuine stuff, boy, genuine stuff'.

Reeling drunk, late that sabbath, he crashed through his kitchen door, onwards to his bedroom. Then he saw her.

They have a way of saying in the argot of Sophiatown, 'Cook out of the head!' signifying that someone was impacted with such violent shock that whatever whiffs of alcohol still wandered through his head were instantaneously evaporated and the man stood sober before stark reality.

There she lay, curled, as if just before she died she begged for a little love, implored some implacable lover to cuddle her a little . . . just this once . . . just this once more.

In screwish anguish, Philemon cried, 'Tilly!'

TEN-TO-TEN

The curfew proper for all Africans in Marabastad, Pretoria, was 10 p.m. By that hour every African, man, woman and child, had to be indoors, preferably in bed; if the police caught you abroad without a 'special permit' you were hauled off to the battleship-grey little police station in First Avenue, near the Aapies River, and clapped in jail. The following morning you found yourself trembling before a magistrate in one of those out-rooms that served as a court, and after a scathing lecture, you were fined ten-bob. So it behove everyone, every black mother's son, to heed that bell and be off the streets at ten.

But it was strange how the first warning bell at ten-to-ten exercised a power of panic among us, really out of all proportion. I suppose, watchless at night, when that bell went off and you were still streets away from your house, you did not know whether it was the first warning – ten-to-ten – giving you that much grace to hurry you on, or the fatal ten o'clock bell itself.

However, there were ever women in their yards, peering over corrugated-iron fences and bedstead gates, calling in sing-song voices, 'Ten-to-ten! Ten-to-ten!' as if the sound of the bell at the police station down there in First Avenue was itself echoed, street after street, urging the belated on, homewards, bedwards, safe from the Law.

As the first bell rang, one Saturday night, a huge African policeman roused himself from the barracks. He was enormous. Nearer seven feet than six feet tall, he towered over his fellow men like a sheer mountain above the mites in the valley. Perfectly formed, his shoulders were like boulders, his arms like the trunks of elephants, the muscles hard and corded. His legs bore his magnificent torso like sturdy pillars under some granite superstructure. He had the largest foot in Pretoria, size 15, and people used to say, 'His boot is special made from the factory'. He was coal-black, with the shiny blackness of ebony, but had large, rolling, white eyes and thick, bluish lips.

He gave a last, critical scrutiny to his shining, black boots and black uniform with tinny buttons, before he stepped into the charge office to report for duty. His was the night-beat. Every night at ten o'clock he went out with one or two other policemen to roam the slummy streets of Marabastad Location and clear them of vagrants. People looked at him with awe; nobody ever argued with him; when his immense shadow fell across you, you shrivelled, or, if you had any locomotion left in you, you gave way fast.

They called him Ten-to-Ten because of that night beat of his, and he was known by no other name. Ten-to-Ten's strength was prodigious and there were many legends in the location about him...

There was the one that he originally came from Tzaneen in Northern Transvaal to seek work in Pretoria. One day he was sitting in a drinking house when a young location hooligan came in and molested the daughter of the house. The girl's father tried to protest but the young hooligan slapped him across the face and told him to shut up. Ten-to-Ten was not accustomed to such behaviour, so he rose from the corner where he was sitting with his tin of beer and walked up to the young man.

'Look,' he said, 'You can't go on like this in another man's house. Please go away now.' He gently pushed the young man towards the door. 'Come on, now, go home.'

The young man swung round with a curse, hesitated a moment as he saw the great bulk of the man confronting him, then with a sneer drew a knife.

They say you can pester a Venda from the North, you can insult him, you can humiliate him in public or cheat him in private, but there are two things you just cannot do with impunity: take his girl, or draw a knife on him.

That night, Ten-to-Ten went jungle-mad.

'Ha!' he snarled.

The knife flashed and caught him in the forearm, blood spurting. But before the young man could withdraw it, Ten-to-Ten had caught him by the neck and dragged him out of the house. In the yard there was the usual corrugated-iron fence. Swinging the boy like wet laundry, Ten-to-Ten lashed him at the fence repeatedly until the fence broke down. Then he started strangling him. Men came running out of the houses. They tried to tear Ten-to-Ten off the boy, but he shook them off like flakes. Soon, somebody sounded a whistle, the call for the police. By the time they came Ten-to-Ten was wielding and hurling all sorts of at-hand weapons at the small crowd that sought to protect the boy.

The police stormed him and knocked him over, bludgeoning him with batons. They managed to manacle his wrists while he was down on his back, then they stepped back wiping the sweat off and waiting for him to rise. Ten-to-Ten rose slowly on one knee. He looked at the police and smiled. The white sergeant was still saying, 'Now, now, come quietly, no more trouble, eh?' when Ten-to-Ten spotted his enemy staggering from the crowd.

He made a savage grunt and, looking at his bound hands, he wrenched them apart and snapped the iron manacles like cotton twine. The police had to rush him again while the crowd scattered.

They say the desk sergeant at the police station decided that day to make Ten-to-Ten a policeman, and Marabastad became a peaceful location.

That is the kind of story you do not have to believe to enjoy.

Another time, legend continues, the coal-delivery man had some difficulty with his horse. He had a one-man horse-cart with which he delivered coal from door to door. On that occasion, the horse suddenly shied, perhaps having been pelted by mischievous boys with slings, and went dashing down the narrow avenue, scattering women with water tins on their heads. Just then Ten-to-Ten came round the corner. He caught the bridle of the horse and struggled to keep it still, being carried along a few yards himself. The horse reared and threatened to break away. Then Ten-to-Ten kicked it with his size 15 boot under the heart. The horse sagged, rolled over and died.

But it was not only for his violent exploits that we thrilled to him. Ten-to-Ten played soccer for the Police First Eleven, he played right full-back. For a giant his size he was remarkably swift, but it was his antics we loved. He would drop an oncoming ball dead before his own goal-posts, and as the opponent's poor forward came rushing at him, he would quickly shift aside with the ball at the last moment, leaving the forward to go hurtling on his own momentum through the goal-posts. Derisively, he would call, 'Goal!' and the excited spectators would shout, 'Ten-to-Ten! Ten-to-Ten!'

Sometimes he would approach the ball ferociously with his

rivals all about it, and he would make as if he was going to blast them ball and all. They would scuttle for cover, only to find that he had stopped the ball and was standing with one foot on it, grinning happily.

When he *did* elect to kick it, he had such powerful shots that the ball went from one end of the field to the other. Once, they say, he took a penalty kick. The ball went with such force that when the goalie tried to stop it, his hands were flayed and the deflected ball still went on to tear a string in the net.

'Ten-to-Ten!'

Yes, he had a sense of humour; and he was also the understanding kind. He knew about his great strength and seldom exercised it recklessly.

In Marabastad of those days there was a very quarrelsome little fellow called Shorty. He was about four-feet six, but as they say, 'He buys tickey's beer and makes a pound's worth of trouble.' No-one but Shorty every really took his tantrums seriously, but people enjoyed teasing him for fun.

'Shorty,' they once told him, 'Ten-to-Ten's in that house telling people that you're not a man, but just a sample.' Shorty boiled over. He strutted into the house with the comic little footsteps of the very short and found Ten-to-Ten sitting with a tin of beer in his hands.

He kicked the tin of beer out of Ten-to-Ten's hands, nearly toppling himself over in the process, and shouted, 'A sample of a man, eh? I'll teach you to respect your betters. Come outside and fight.' The others quickly signalled Ten-to-Ten that it was all a joke and he caught on. But Shorty was so aggrieved that he pestered Ten-to-Ten all afternoon.

At last Ten-to-Ten, tired of the sport, rose, lifted Shorty bodily off the ground and carried him down the street with a procession of cheering people behind them. Shorty was raging; he threw futile punches at Ten-to-Ten's chest. His dangling legs were kicking about furiously, but Ten-to-Ten carried him all the way to the police station.

It was a startled desk sergeant who suddenly found a midget landed on his desk, shouting, 'I'll kill him! I'll kill him!'

'What's this?' the sergeant wanted to know.

Wearily, Ten-to-Ten explained, 'He says he wants to give me a fair fight.'

Shorty was fined ten-bob, and when he came out of there, he turned to Ten-to-Ten disgustedly, and spat, 'Coward!'

Ten-to-Ten walked with two other policemen, Constables Masemola and Ramokgopa, up First Avenue into glittering Boom Street. It was like suddenly walking out of an African slum into a chunk of the Orient. They strolled slowly up the tarred Boom Street, past the Empire Cinema. Now and then they would stop to look at the exotic foods in the window of some Indian shop and the pungent smells of eastern cooking and eastern toiletry would rise to their nostrils. Ahead, a hundred yards ahead, you could see the Africans who had no special permits to be out at night sorting themselves from the Indian and Coloured night-crowds and dodging down some dark streets. They had long noticed the stalwart shadow of Ten-to-Ten coming up. He knew it too, but did not bother.

He reasoned inside himself that as long as they were scampering home, it was a form of respect for the Law. Unlike some of the other policemen who ferreted out Africans and delighted in chasing them down the road, to him, even when he caught one or two on the streets at night, it was enough to say, 'You there, home!' and as they fled before him his duty felt done.

Then they turned into the dark of Second Avenue of the location, away from where their eyes were guided by the blinking neons, into the murky streets where only their feet found the familiar way. It was silent, but Ten-to-Ten knew the residents were around, the silence was only because he was there. He was walking down the street, a presence that suddenly hushed these normally noisy people. In fact, he had heard their women as he entered the street calling down along it, 'Ten-to-Ten! Ten-to-Ten!'

It was not like the adulatory cheering on the soccer field, this calling of 'Ten-to-Ten!' This one had a long, dreary, plaintive note . . . to carry it far along the street? or to express heart-felt agony? In the field he felt their pride in him, the admiration for his wonderful physique, his skill and his sense of humour. The rapport between himself and his spectators who lined the field was delicious. There even the puniest of them would rush into the field after he had scored a goal, slap him on the back happily, and say, 'Ai, but you, you Ten-to-Ten.'

He would come off the field and find a hero-worshipping youngster carrying his coat and pants to him, and another pushing his glittering Hercules bicycle. The small boy would push out his robin chest and yell, 'Ten-to-Ten!' unselfconsciously.

But here, people skulked behind tin shacks and wailed their misery at whatever perverse god crushed them, round about the hour of ten. Some of them were probably muttering in whispers even now as he passed. Had he not seen lower down the street a light suddenly go out in a house? It was probably a drinking house where they sat in the dark with their calabashes and tins trying to find their 'blind mouthes', with the auntie of the house hissing importunately, 'Simeon shut up, you fool, don't you know it's Ten-to-Ten?'

They passed a church and fancied they heard a rustling sound in the porch. They went to investigate. Out and past them bolted a boy and a girl. He mocked his shock after them, 'What, even in the House of the Lord!' They ran faster.

Fifth Street was empty and dark but before long they heard familiar grunting sounds. Ten-to-Ten signalled the other policemen to walk quietly. Off the street, hidden in an opening among tall grass, was a group of dice-players. They had formed a ring, inside which the candle was shielded from the breezes. The thrower would retreat a little from the ring, and shaking his dice in his bowled fist take a lunge forward, and cast them into the patch of light, giving a visceral grunt to coax his luck. Coins of the stake were lying in the centre.

Creeping low, Ten-to-Ten and his mates tip-toed up to them. They were so intent on the game that they heard nothing until suddenly he rose to his great height, like Mephistopheles out of the gloom, and bellowed, 'Ten-to-Ten!'

They splashed in all directions. One boy jumped into Ten-to-Ten and bounced back, falling to the ground. A policeman put a boot on his shoulder with just enough pressure to keep him there. Another chap never even got up, a rough hand had caught him by the neck. The boy who had nursed the candle tried to get away faster than his body would allow him and his feet kept slipping under him in his haste like a panicking dog's on a hard, smooth floor. He whimpered pointlessly, 'It's not me! It's not me!'

Ten-to-Ten just roared with Olympian laughter, 'Haw! Haw! Haw!'

When the boy finally took ground, he catapulted away. The other policemen brought the two detainees up to Ten-to-Ten; he did not trouble to question them, just re-lit the candle and held it in their frightened faces.

Then he said, 'Search them, Masemola. You know I'm only interested in knives.'

Constable Masemola searched them but found no knives. In the pocket of one he found a little tin containing a condom. He held it up to Ten-to-Ten like the finger of a glove. 'Sies!' said Ten-to-Ten disgustedly, brushing aside Masemola's hand. Then to the boys, 'Off with you!' and they crashed through the tall grass into the location.

The other constable had picked up the coins from the ground, and while Masemola was still wondering aloud what those boys thought they knew about the use of condoms, Ten-to-Ten noticed the other constable pocketing the coins. Again, he just said, 'Sies!'

They went up Third Avenue, Ten-to-Ten thinking thoughts for which he could find no words . . . .

'Am I, perhaps, the only fool in this job? All the other policemen take bribes, intimidate shopkeepers, force half-guilt-conscious women to go to bed with them. Some beat up people needlessly, a few actually seem to enjoy the wanton slap, the unprovoked blow, the unreturnable kick for their own selves. Of course, it's seldom necessary for me to hit anybody. Before my bulk the runts fly. Maybe that's why. Maybe if I was little like these chaps I'd also want to push people around.

'But, really, you should hear these policemen grumble when

the white sergeant barks at them in the charge office. Then they know they're black; that the whiteman is unreasonable, unjust, bossy, a bastard. But, God! See these chaps in the location on the beat. They treat their own people like ordure. And when the whiteman is with us on the beat, they surpass themselves. Damn that Ramokgopa! I felt so ashamed the other day when he hit a hopeless drunk with a baton until Sergeant du Toit said, "That's enough, now, Ramokgopa." God, I felt ashamed! The blackman strikes, the whiteman says, "That's enough, now".

'And this business of making women sleep with you because you caught them with a drum of illicit beer. I can't understand it. If I want a piece of bottom – and, by God, now and then the fierce, burning pang stabs me, too – then I want the woman to want me too, to come alive under me, not to lie there like a dead fish. The thing's rape, man, however much she consented.

'What do I want in this job, anyway. It's a bastard of a job. Funny hours, low pay, strange orders that make no sense, violence, ever violence, and the daily spectacle of the degradation of my people. Well, I suppose it's a job. Otherwise, I'd be with those workless fellows we corner every day, and arrest for not having passes. Hell, if I hadn't taken this job, I'm sure I'd be in jail now. Jail? God, me, I'd long ago have been hanged for murder if some policeman handled me as our chaps manhandle these poor devils.

'But I have to work. I came here to work because I like to work. No, because back home in Tzaneen the people are starving, the rains haven't come these many years and the land is crying out, giving up the vain struggle to live – to push up one, little green blade, to justify herself – she lies just there like a barren, passionless woman seeing men hunger and die. No, but really because Mapula is waiting for me. Mapula? Ahhh! The memory stings me and I feel the subtle, nameless pain that only a big man knows. I can't cry . . . I can't cry . . .'

They came out of the location, again into Boom Street whose bright lights seemed to crackle into his twilight consciousness. They came out on to the bicycle shop.

A bicycle shop was supposed to repair bicycles and sell spare parts for them and there was always an upturned bicycle, one or other wheel missing, allegedly in the process of repair, outside the shop or at night in the window. But in Marabastad it was more of a music shop where the most raucous, the screechiest, the bansheest, the bawdiest cacophonies of township jazz bawled and caterwauled from the 78's inside to loudspeakers outside. 'We-Selina, go greet me your ma!' shrieked the lonesome son-in-law loud enough for his sweetheart, Selina, or indeed the mother-in-law herself, to hear him back in the Reserves.

Ten-to-Ten looked at his pocket-watch. Twenty-to-twelve. Odd, he thought, here was a Coloured girl dancing to music that was distinctly African township jazz – this chance thought was soon dispersed by the sight of the crowds that spilled from the Empire Cinema. Most of them were well-dressed Indian men with lovely Coloured girls; there were few Indian girls. A sprinkling of African men were in the crowd, but from their unalarmed expressions one could easily see that they had been to school and had the 'papers'.

As they strolled along the pavement the policemen saw an old Zulu, clad in a greenish-khaki military overcoat, huddling over a glowing brazier. He was the *Matshingilane* – the nightwatchman. It was not clear which building he was guarding; probably several Indian bosses had chipped in to get him to look after the whole row of buildings. Lucky devil! Most times he slept well, safe in the knowledge that a policeman on the beat would stroll up and down watching the buildings for him.

'*Poisa! Poisa!* – Police! Police! They're killing an African man down there!'

Ten-to-Ten and his mates dashed down the street. They found a crowd of Indians pummelling a young African man. Ten-to-Ten barged into them like a bulldozer, pushing the crowd this way and that, until he got to the man on the ground.

'What's going on here?' he barked.

Scores of voices replied, 'He's a thief!'

'A pickpocket!'

'The lady's handbag!'

'He hit the gentleman first!'

'He bumped him!'

'And swore at him!'

'He's always robbing people!'

'We know him! We know him!'

Ten-to-Ten lifted the African from the ground. The man cowered before the enormous form over him.

'Well?' Ten-to-Ten asked.

'They lie,' was all the man could say for himself.

Somebody tried to grab at him but Ten-to-Ten pushed him away and pulled the victim towards himself, more protectively, saying, 'No, you don't.'

Then he addressed the crowd, 'Look here, I'm going to arrest this man and no-one is going to take him away from me. No-one, you hear?' He was quiet for a moment and looked around challengingly. Then he continued, 'Now, is there anybody who cares to lay a charge against him?'

There were murmurings, but no definite charge. Someone called out, weakly, 'But he's a thief.'

Ten-to-Ten said, 'All right, come forward and lay a charge.'

Instead, a hand again reached for the man. Ten-to-Ten released his charge for a moment to go after the owner of the hand, a half-impulsive movement.

'Look out!' someone yelled, and the crowd surged away. Ten-to-Ten spun round and saw that the African had drawn a long-bladed knife.

'Aw-right, come for me, you bastards!' he growled.

The savage blood leapt inside Ten-to-Ten. He lunged at the man like a black flash. If the knife had been shorter, he would have got it in the neck, but it was unwieldy and only slashed him across the shoulder.

'Ah!' soughed the fascinated crowd.

Ten-to-Ten caught the man's knife-arm at the wrist and above the elbow, then brought it down on his upthrust knee. Crack! It snapped like a dry twig.

The sharp shriek curdled the night air and the knife went clattering to the pavement. The man went down to the ground, whining, and the fury passed out of Ten-to-Ten.

Quietly, he said to the man, 'I could have killed you for that ... knife.'

The crowd broke up in little groups into the night.

Ten-to-Ten said to Masemola, with a careless wave of the hand, 'Take him to de la Rey. I'm coming.'

He stood thinking, 'This was my bad night, the young, bloody fool!'

THE DUBE TRAIN

The morning was too cold for a summer morning, at least, to me, a child of the sun. But then on all Monday mornings I feel rotten and shivering, with a clogged feeling in the chest and a nauseous churning in the stomach. It debilitates my interest in the whole world around me.

The Dube Station with the prospect of congested trains, filled with sour-smelling humanity, did not improve my impression of a hostile life directing its malevolence plumb at me. All sorts of disgruntledties darted through my brain: the lateness of the trains, the shoving savagery of the crowds, the grey aspect around me. Even the announcer over the loudspeaker gave confused directions. I suppose it had something to do with the peculiar chemistry of the body on Monday morning. But for me all was wrong with the world.

Yet, by one of those flukes that occur in all routines, the train I caught was not full when it came. I usually try to avoid seats next to the door, but sometimes it cannot be helped. So it was that Monday morning when I hopped into the Third Class carriage. As the train moved off, I leaned out of the paneless window and looked lack-lustrely at the leaden platform churning away beneath me like a fast conveyer belt.

Two or three yards away, a door had been broken and repaired with masonite so that it would be an opening door no more. Moreover, just there a seat was missing, and there was a kind of a hall.

I was sitting opposite a hulk of a man; his hugeness was obtrusive to the sight when you saw him, and to the mind when you looked away. His head tilted to one side in a half-drowsy position, with flaring nostrils and trembling lips. He looked like a kind of genie, pretending to sleep but watching your every nefarious intention. His chin was stubbled with crisp, little black barbs. The neck was thick and corded, and the enormous chest was a live barrel that heaved forth and back. The overall he wore was open almost down to the navel, and he seemed to have nothing else underneath. I stared, fascinated, at his large breasts with their winking, dark nipples.

With the rocking of the train as it rolled towards Phefeni Station, he swayed slightly this way and that, and now and then he lazily chanted a township ditty. The titillating bawdiness of the words incited no humour or lechery or significance. The words were words, the tune was just a tune.

Above and around him, the other passengers, looking Monday-bleared, had no enthusiasm about them. They were just like the lights of the carriage – dull, dreary, undramatic. Almost as if they, too, felt that they should not be alight during the day.

Phefeni Station rushed at us with human faces blurring past. When the train stopped, in stepped a girl. She must have been a mere child. Not just *petite*, but juvenile in structure. Yet her manner was all adult as if she knew all about 'this sorry scheme of things entire' and with a scornful toss relegated it. She had the premature features of the township girls, pert, arrogant, live. There was that air about her that petrified any grown-ups who might think of asking for her seat. She sat next to me.

The train slid into Phomolong. Against the red-brick waiting-room I saw a *tsotsi* lounging, for all the world not a damn interested in taking the train, but I knew the type, so I watched him in grim anticipation. When the train started sailing out of the platform, he turned round nonchalantly and trippled along backwards towards an open door. It amazes me no end how these boys know exactly where the edge of the platform comes when they run like that backwards. Just at the drop he caught the ledge of the train and heaved himself in gracefully.

He swaggered towards us and stood between our seats with his back to the outside, his arms gripping the frame of the paneless window. He noticed the girl and started teasing her. All township love-making is rough.

'*Hi*, rubberneck!' – he clutched at her pear-like breast jutting from her sweater – 'how long did you think you'll duck me?'

She looked round in panic; at me, at the old lady opposite her, at the hulk of a man opposite me. Then she whimpered, 'Ah, *Au-boetie*, I don't even know you.'

The *tsotsi* snarled, 'You don't know me, eh? You don't know me when you're sitting with your student friends. You don't know last night, too, *nê*? You don't know how you ducked me?'

Some woman, reasonably out of reach, murmured, 'The children of today . . .' in a drifting sort of way.

Mzimhlophe, the dirty-white station.

The *tsotsi* turned round and looked out of the window on to the platform. He recognized some of his friends there and hailed them.

'O, Zigzagza, it's how there?'

'It's jewish!'

'*Hela*, Tholo, my ma hears me, I want that ten-'n-six!'

'Go get it in hell!'

'Weh, my sister, don't lissen to that guy. Tell him Shakespeare nev'r said so!'

The gibberish exchange was all in exuberant superlatives.

The train left the platform in the echoes of its stridency. A washer-woman had just got shoved into it by ungallant males, bundle and all. People in the train made sympathetic noises, but too many passengers had seen too many tragedies to be rattled by this incident. They just remained bleared.

As the train approached New Canada, the confluence of the Orlando and the Dube train lines, I looked over the head of the girl next to me. It must have been a crazy engineer who had designed this crossing. The Orlando train comes from the right. It crosses the Dube train overhead just before we reach New Canada. But when it reaches the station it is on the right again, for the Johannesburg train enters extreme left. It is a curious kind of game.

Moreover, it has necessitated cutting the hill and building a bridge. But just this quirk of an engineer's imagination has left a spectacularly beautiful scene. After the drab, chocolate-box houses of the township, monotonously identical row upon row, this gash of man's imposition upon nature never fails to intrigue me.

Our caveman lover was still at the girl while people were changing from our train to the Westgate train in New Canada. The girl wanted to get off, but the *tsotsi* would not let her. When the train left the station, he gave her a vicious slap across the face so that her beret went flying. She flung a leg over me and rolled across my lap in her hurtling escape. The *tsotsi* followed, and as he passed me he reeled with the sway of the train.

To steady himself, he put a full paw in my face. It smelled sweaty-sour. Then he ploughed through the humanity of the train, after the girl. Men gave way shamelessly, but one woman would not take it. She burst into a spitfire tirade that whiplashed at the men.

'Lord, you call yourself men, you poltroons! You let a small ruffian insult you. Fancy, he grabs at a girl in front of you – might be your daughter – this thing with the manner of a pig! If there were real men here, they'd pull his pants off and give him such a leathering he'd never sit down for a week. But, no, you let him do this here; tonight you'll let him do it in your homes. And all you do is whimper, "The children of today have never no respect!" *Sies!*'

The men winced. They said nothing, merely looked round at each other in shy embarrassment. But those barbed words had brought the little thug to a stop. He turned round, scowled at the woman, and with cold calculation cursed her anatomically, twisting his lips to give the word the full measure of its horror.

It was like the son of Ham finding a word for his awful discovery. It was like an impression that shuddered the throne of God Almighty. It was both a defilement and a defiance.

'Helá, you street-urchin, that woman is your mother,' came the shrill voice of the big hulk of a man, who had all the time sat quietly opposite me, humming his lewd little township ditty. Now he moved towards where the *tsotsi* stood rooted.

There was menace in every swing of his clumsy movements, and the half-mumbled tune of his song sounded like under-breath cursing for all its calmness. The carriage froze into silence.

Suddenly, the woman shrieked and men scampered on to seats. The *tsotsi* had drawn a sheath-knife, and he faced the big man.

There is something odd that a knife does to various people in a crowd. Most women go into pointless clamour, sometimes even hugging round the arms the men who might fight for them. Some men make gangway, stampeding helter-skelter; but with that hulk of man the sight of the gleaming blade in the *tsotsi*'s hand, drove him beserk. The splashing people left a sort of arena. There was an evil leer in his eye, much as if he was experiencing satanic satisfaction.

Croesus Cemetery flashed past.

Seconds before the impact, the *tsotsi* lifted the blade and plunged it obliquely. Like an instinctual, predatory beast, he seemed to know exactly where the vulnerable jugular was and he aimed for it. The jerk of the train deflected his stroke, though, and the blade slit a long cleavage down the big man's open chest.

With a demoniacal scream, the big man reached out for the boy crudely, careless now of the blade that made another gash in his arm. He caught the boy by the upper arm with the left hand, and between the legs with the right and lifted him bodily. Then he hurled him towards me. The flight went clean through the paneless window, and only a long cry trailed in the wake of the rushing train.

It was so sudden that the passengers were galvanized into action, darting to the windows; the human missile was nowhere to be seen. It was not a fight proper, not a full-blown quarrel. It was just an incident in the morning Dube train.

The big man, bespattered with blood, got off at Langlaagte Station. Only after we had left the station did the stunned passengers break out into a cacophony of chattering.

Odd, that no one expressed sympathy for the boy or man. They were just greedily relishing the thrilling episode of the morning.

THE WILL TO DIE

I have heard much, have read much more, of the Will to Live; stories of fantastic retreats from the brink of death at moments when all hope was lost. To the aid of certain personalities in the bleakest crises, spiritual resources seem to come forward from what? Character? Spirit? Soul? Or the Great Reprieve of a Spiritual Clemency – hoisting them back from the muddy slough of the Valley of the Shadow.

But the Will to Die has intrigued me more . . .

I have also heard that certain snakes can hypnotize their victim, a rat, a frog or a rabbit, not only so that it cannot flee to safety in the overwhelming urge for survival, but so that it is even attracted towards its destroyer, and appears to enjoy dancing towards its doom. I have often wondered if there is not some mesmeric power that Fate employs to engage some men deliberately, with macabre relishment, to seek their destruction and to plunge into it.

Take Foxy . . .

His real name was Philip Matauoane, but for some reason, I think from the excesses of his college days, everybody called him Foxy. He was a teacher in a small school in Barberton, South Africa. He had been to Fort Hare University College in the Cape Province, and had majored in English (with distinction) and Native Administration. Then he took the University Education Diploma (teaching) with Rhodes University, Grahamstown.

He used to say, 'I'm the living exemplar of the modern, educated African's dilemma. I read English and trained to be a teacher – the standard profession for my class those days; but you never know which government department is going to expel you and pitchfork you into which other government department. So I also took Native Administration as a safety device.'

You would think that that labels the cautious, providential kind of human.

Foxy was a short fellow, the type that seems in youth to rush forward towards old age, but somewhere, around the eve of middle-age, stops dead and ages no further almost forever. He had wide, owlish eyes and a trick with his mouth that suggested withering contempt for all creation. He invariably wore clothes that swallowed him: the coat overflowed and drowned his arms, the trousers sat on his chest in front and billowed obscenely behind. He was a runt of a man.

But in that unlikely body resided a live, restless brain.

When Foxy first left college, he went to teach English at Barberton High School. He was twenty-five then, and those were the days when high school pupils were just ripe to provoke or prejudice a young man of indifferent morals. He fell in love with a young girl, Betty Kumalo, his own pupil.

I must explain this spurious phenomenon of 'falling in love'. Neither Foxy nor Betty had the remotest sense of commitment to the irrelevance of marrying some day. The society of the times was such that affairs of this nature occurred easily. Parents did not mind much. Often they would invite a young teacher to the home, and as soon as he arrived, would eclipse themselves, leaving the daughter with stern but unmistakable injunctions to 'be hospitable to the teacher'.

We tried to tell Foxy, we his fellow-teachers, that this arrangement was too nice to be safe, but these things had been written in the stars.

Foxy could not keep away from Betty's home. He could not be discreet. He went there every day, every unblessed day. He took her out during week-ends and they vanished into the country-side in his ancient Chevrolet.

On Mondays he would often say to me, 'I don't know what's wrong with me. I know this game is dangerous. I know Betty will destroy me, but that seems to give tang to the adventure. Hopeless. Hopeless,' and he would throw his arms out.

I had it out with him once.

'Foxy,' I said, 'you must stop this nonsense. It'll ruin you.'

There came a glint of pleasure, real ecstasy it seemed to me, into his eyes. It was as if the prospect of ruin was hallelujah.

He said to me, 'My intelligence tells me that it'll ruin me, but there's a magnetic force that draws me to that girl, and another part of me, much stronger than intelligence, just simply exults.'

'Marry her, then, and get done with it.'

'No!' He said it so vehemently that I was quite alarmed. 'Something in me wants that girl pregnant but not a wife.'

I thought it was a hysterical utterance.

You cannot go flinging wild oats all over a fertile field, not even wild weeds. It had to happen.

If you are a school-teacher, you can only get out of a situation like that if you marry the girl, that is if you value your job. Foxy promptly married – another girl! But he was smart enough to give Betty's parents £50. That, in the hideous system of *lobola*, the system of bride-price, made Betty his second wife. And no authority on earth could accuse him of seduction.

But when his wife found out about it, she battered him, as the Americans would say, 'To hell and back.'

Foxy started drinking heavily.

Then another thing began to happen; Foxy got drunk during working hours. Hitherto, he had been meticulous about not cultivating one's iniquities in the teeth of one's job, but now he seemed to be splashing in the gutter with a will.

I will never forget the morning another teacher and I found him stinkingly drunk about half-an-hour before school was to start. We forced him into a shebeen and asked the queen to let him sleep it off. We promised to make the appropriate excuses to the headmaster on his behalf. Imagine our consternation when he came reeling into the assembly hall where we were saying morning prayers with all the staff and pupils. How I prayed that morning!

These things happen. Everybody noticed Foxy's condition,

except, for some reason, the headmaster. We hid him in the Biology Laboratory for the better part of the day, but that did not make the whole business any more edifying. Happily, he made his appearance before we could perjure ourselves to the headmaster. Later, however, we learned that he had told the shebeen-queen that he would go to school perforce because we other teachers were trying to get him into trouble for absence from work and that we wished to 'outshine' him. Were we livid?

Every one of his colleagues gave him a dressing down. We told him that no more was he alone in this: it involved the dignity of us all. The whole location was beginning to talk nastily about us. Moreover, there was a violent, alcoholic concoction brewed in the location called Barberton. People just linked 'Barberton', 'High' and 'School' to make puns about us.

Superficially, it hurt him to cause us so much trouble, but something deep down in him did not allow him really to care. He went on drinking hard. His health was beginning to crack under it. Now, he met every problem with the gurgling answer of the bottle.

One night, I heard that he was very ill, so I went to see him at home. His wife had long since given him up for lost; they no more even shared a bedroom. I found him in his room. The scene was ghastly. He was lying in his underwear in bed linen which was stained with the blotches of murdered bugs. There was a plate of uneaten food that must have come the day before yesterday. He was breathing heavily. Now and then he tried to retch, but nothing came up. His bloodshot eyes rolled this way and that, and whenever some respite graciously came, he reached out for a bottle of gin and gulped at it until the fierce liquid poured over his stubbled chin.

He gibbered so that I thought he was going mad. Then he would retch violently again, that jolting, vomitless quake of a retch.

He needed a doctor but he would not have one. His wife carped, 'Leave the pig to perish.'

I went to fetch the doctor, nevertheless. We took quite a while, and when we returned, his wife sneered at us, 'You wouldn't like to see him now.' We went into his room and found him lost in oblivion. A strange girl was lying by his side. In his own house!

I did not see him for weeks, but I heard enough. They said that he was frequenting dangerous haunts. One drunken night he was beaten up and robbed. Another night he returned home stark naked, without a clue as to who had stripped him.

Liquor should have killed him, but some compulsive urge chose differently. After a binge one night, he wandered hopelessly about the darksome location streets, seeking his home. At last, he decided on a gate, a house, a door. He was sure that that was his home. He banged his way in, ignored the four or five men singing hymns in the sitting-room, and staggered into the bedroom. He flung himself on to the bed and hollered, 'Woman, it's time that I sleep in your bed. I'm sick and tired of being a widower with a live wife.'

The men took up sticks and battered Foxy to a pulp. They got it into their heads that the woman of the house had been in the business all the time; that only now had her lover gone and got drunk enough to let the cat out of the bag. They beat the woman, too, within millimetres of her life. All of them landed in jail for long stretches.

But I keep having a stupid feeling that somehow, Philip 'Foxy' Matauoane would have felt: 'This is as it should be.'

Some folks live the obsession of death.

III

REPORTS JOHANNESBURG 1956–7

TERROR IN THE TRAINS

Congestion on the trains has become virtually unbearable during peak hours. The few third-class coaches, the all too few trains, jam-packed with gasping, frightened humanity – oh, what a chance for your criminal stepbrothers.

There is little method in the operations of these criminals. Many pick-pockets just put their hands into your pocket and take what they want. More likely than not you will not feel anything as you struggle for breath in the crowd. If you do, what matter? They out-brave you and threaten you with violence. The younger pick-pockets go down on their knees, cut a hole in your trousers with a razor blade, and then let slide into their hands whatever comes forth.

But the true terror for train users comes from the rough-house thugs who hold people up at the point of a knife or gun, or simply rob and beat them up. The fear among passengers is so deep that some don't even want to admit that they have been robbed. And pay-days – Fridays, month-ends, from half-past four in the afternoon – are the devil's birthdays.

The other day we went to see for ourselves. We got to Park Station about 3 o'clock in the afternoon. People were already beginning to stream in. Almost everyone was in a hurry, and had an anxious expression. It was Friday again. Then we went through the barriers, down the steps, and into the swarms.

Flush on our arrival, plain-clothes policemen were arresting a man for robbing somebody on the platform. They twisted him round, and pushed him off through some cursing people. The drama had begun. We let a few trains pass, for we wanted to see how the people in this thick mass boarded them.

Wheee! In rushed an electric train. A man in brown overalls yelled the destination and the stops on the way, but his voice, already hoarse, couldn't rise above the din. People were jabbing at each other frantically, asking, 'Where is it going? Where does it stop?' Before everyone could get in, the train pulled out. Men and women were hanging precariously outside open doors, squeezing for all they were worth to get in. Then the train slid out of sight. The same thing happened with train after train.

We chanced a Dube train. It was packed, jammed like putty. On all sides humans were pressing against us; in the passage, between seats, on seat-backs – humans. Four on three-men seats, three on two-men seats. Crammed. One woman screamed for help because somebody pressed against her hard and her purse seemed to be sliding out of her pocket. At intermediate stations more and more people forced their way in.

At Phefeni Station many people got off and we had some relief. As the train moved off, in a sparkling flash, I saw a man poised on the platform like a baseball pitcher. Then he flung a missile. Crash! It struck a window. We all ducked. It looked like somebody doing it just out of hatred. Maybe he'd tried to rob people in an earlier train and failed.

Nothing much happened for the rest of the trip – that is nothing except periodic pickpocketing and stealing of parcels which we learned about later. On our way back we met a man who was so drunk that he didn't know that he was being robbed. He got pushed out of the train and landed on his back.

In the coach next to ours three thugs assaulted a man who resisted their attempts to go through his pockets. After this the other passengers were afraid to interfere with the thugs, who robbed a few more people before getting off the train.

We met a man whose suitcase had been thrown out of a window as the train passed a station. He had to get off at the next station and come back to look for it. Wonder of wonders! He found a woman who had taken charge of the suitcase, and he got it back intact. It happened in Johannesburg.

There are various gangs operating on trains or near railway stations on the Reef. In the Moroka-Jabavu-Mofolo area and in Pimville it is mainly the Torch Gang. They specialize in 'Dark Patch' operation – robberies in unlit areas just outside the stations. Suddenly a man finds a torch flashed into his face, blinding him for a moment. Then a stunning blow on the head. Next thing he is lying in the grass, beaten up and robbed.

In the Orlando area there is the Mlamlankunzi Gang, a bunch of youngsters who work in the trains. One will come from behind and give you an elbow lock round the neck. Another will point a knife or a screwdriver to your belly. And then they rob you. If you resist, they throw you out of the running train.

There has been some violent reaction to these train robbers, and *tsotsis* in general, in the Dube area. Propped-eared Zulus first ganged together to beat them up, a natural reaction of harried people at the end of their tether.

But then it went all haywire. Some Zulus went about hitting people indiscriminately. They have a saying, 'Hit a cap and a *tsotsi* will jump out.' So anybody who wore a cap was in danger of being clubbed. Recently they went even further, beating up old women in their homes after saying, 'Your son is a *tsotsi*.' They smashed houses without having done the most elementary research.

Then, a few weeks ago, the situation became electric, and the two main opposing tribes in the area poised themselves for violence. The Zulus, chiefly from Dube Hostel, and the Basotho, with reinforcements from as far as Evaton and Vereeniging, clashed during a bloody week-end of violence. They went at each other with murderous weapons, including battle axes. During three days about forty people were killed and a hundred injured. The police were at it day and night keeping the blood-mad warriors from each other, and sometimes they were forced to shoot.

What caused this sudden violent explosion? In a certain sense, it was not a surprise to those of us who live in these townships. We have lived with terrorism for so long and we have always feared that one day there would be an eruption. You can't live with assault, robbery and murder without something big happening eventually.

The situation has been aggravated, according to many people, by the policy of ethnic grouping, which has led the more tribal among us to think of other tribes as 'foreigners', 'enemies'. We are not allowed to learn to live together in peace, say the train-using, bus-boarding philosophers to whom the Dube wave of terror has become a matter of life and death.

BOOZERS BEWARE OF BARBERTON!

There is a shebeen yard where the people have gone mysteriously mad.

Number 17, Marshall Street, Ferreirastown, Johannesburg, is just about the craziest address I've met. So many people who have lived there have gone mad, even as so many other people have stood in the slummy yard drinking that poisonous brew of shebeen invention – Barberton. There is an obvious connection. But the startling fact is that four of these people lived and went mad in the same room.

A South African neurologist has just sent a paper to America on Barberton. He has found that it does drive certain people mad.

In the 1940's, they say, a Coloured woman living in this yard and selling Barberton, thought that her neighbours might want to take away from her her profitable trade in shebeen liquor. So in the dead of night she decided to 'put the jinx' on this room, and here and there in the yard, by planting magic. Not long after this people began to behave strangely.

That's their story of how it all started, but the facts of what happened subsequently are hardly less startling. At about this time there lived in the fatal room, Chris Tyssen, his wife and Willem Tyssen, his brother. Chris just suddenly found out that his wife was unhappy with him. They were always quarrelling and fighting, until one day she just deserted him to go and live in Pretoria. This affected Chris so badly that he became very ill, and sometimes would mutter delirious nonsense. Then suddenly his brother, Willem, started to act crazy. This was more serious than Chris's condition which was described as having had 'just a touch'. Willem did mad things like collecting bits of paper, old tins, rubbish. Then suddenly he vanished. People looked for him everywhere. Not a sign of him. Not a sound about him. For over two months. Then came the rumour that an unidentified body had been found at Germiston. He had been drowned in a lake. The police did not suspect foul play, but his friends are still uneasy. He was given a pauper's funeral.

Chris was ejected from the room, but he still stays in the yard, sleeping outside on a miserable mattress with the stars for a blanket. He wanders in and out like a lost, bewildered animal.

Just opposite this notorious room is the Fourie room. Here lived Willie 'Oom Johnnie' Fourie and his wife, Maria. Unlike many of the other victims, Oom Johnnie did not get ill at all. He was completely healthy on the night of March 17, 1957, when he suddenly got it into his head that he wanted to make a speech. He stripped himself stark naked, grabbed an axe and jumped on to the table to deliver his great oration. He made a magnificent figure standing there in his innocence and the light casting an enormous, distorted shadow on the wall and roof.

The people rushed out and sent for the Flying Squad. He was removed and taken to the 'mad cells' at Newlands Police Station where he was duly garbed in a blanket and left among the other mixed-ups. His wife, Maria, went to see him on the following Thursday. He seemed all right. But when she went to see him again, she heard that he had died.

Whom God would destroy He first sends mad.

The wife has been so distracted by the death of Oom Johnnie, that she's now a thin edge away herself from daylight clear level-headedness. She moves about in a daze and mumbles, 'Me, I don't want to talk. I don't want to talk. I don't want to talk.'

But the yard in which she lives has become the talk of Malay Camp (Ferreirastown). And in that Doom Room, now occupied by two brothers, it looks like violence plans to strike again. Now, these two brothers are very fond of each other. The other day they had been having a brotherly drink together. They got a little high. When they got home the elder brother just suddenly attacked his kid brother. They had a wild fight, throwing in everything they could lay hands on, kicking, biting, fisting. They smashed two of the large window panes of the Doom Room. By the following day when I got there they had contracted a sulky truce, and it was obvious there was no longer as much bad blood between them. But the people in the yard intimated to me in hushed whispers that they knew it was the jinx over the room striking again.

I think, however, there is a much simpler explanation. Next to Maria Fourie's room there's another room whose role in this business is much more ominous than people realize. This is the room where they sell Barberton in a big way. African men come from the neighbouring mines, the town, and industrial concerns for their mugful of *Mbamba*. But Barberton is a poison made in such a way as to give a quick kick. It is made of bread, yeast and sugar. Its main characteristic is that it is 'raw' (swiftly prepared) liquor. One of its commonest effects is upon the skin which it peels off and sallows. People get red lips and purulent black pimples on the face. But it has made those who have drunk it for a long time raging madmen, especially in fights. Here then may lie the answer to the mystery of the yard of lunatics. Some people have fed too long, and too much on a poisonous concoction. It has made them sick and driven them mad.

BROTHERS IN CHRIST

Mr Drum walks into colour-bar churches

I visited several churches, English and Afrikaans, in and around Johannesburg. I went to Irene, a Dutch Reformed Church, in Quarter Street.

I walked through a side door into the body of the church and sat down. The service had started. There was no comment, though, after the service as I walked out, there was some whispering.

My next visit took me to the Central Methodist Church in Kruis Street. A church official with a smile on his face asked me to go to the gallery as, he said, the hall downstairs was full. But there were many empty seats downstairs. The following Sunday I went to the Nederduits Gereformeerde of Hervormde Kerk (D.R.C.) Bez. Valley. Youths who were sitting in a pew motioned for me not to sit next to them. I moved their Bibles aside and sat down; then they edged away until a good three feet separated us. Somebody in the pew behind me patted me on the back and said, 'This is a white church, you can't be in here. You must go.' I turned round to face him, then he and his friend yanked me to my feet and led me out of the church. Outside, their Christian calm returned to them, and they explained to me that I should go to 'my own church'.

The Presbyterian Church in Noord Street allowed me in, yet the one in Orange Grove refused me admittance. They explained that the hall was rented from some boys' club whose policy did not allow Non-whites into the hall. They also said something about the laws of the country.

At the Kensington D.R.C. Gemeente, an aged church official was just about to close the doors when he saw me. He bellowed in Afrikaans: '*What soek jy?*' (What do you want?)

'I've come to church,' I said.

He shoved me violently, shouting for me to get away. I walked off dejected. A few yards away was the Baptist Church, and as I walked towards it I began to think that people didn't want me to share their church. As I walked through the Baptist door I was tensed, waiting for that tap on the shoulder . . . but instead I was given a hymn book and welcomed into the church. I sat through the service.

At the Fairview Gemeente of the Assemblies of God the welcome party at the door invited me in but offered me a seat at the back. Everybody was polite, very Christian, and wanted to know where I came from. This up and down treatment wasn't doing my nerves much good. The previous day, at the Claim Street

Seventh Day Adventist Church, I had been stopped at the church door and told I could not go in. Then a church official thought that perhaps I could be placed somewhere at the back, but another was definitely against it. So I turned away. A week or two later I went again and was asked to sit at the back. Later I was asked to leave. 'We object to your presence,' said a large white man.

On yet another Sunday I went to the D.R.C. Church, Langlaagte, Johannesburg, in the company of a photographer. I walked up the pathway to the door of the church where I was stopped by a young European usher. I explained to him that I wanted to attend the service.

'But this is a church for whites only. Why don't you go to one of your own churches?' the usher said. He hesitated for a while, then he took me round the side of the church, and made me wait outside while he consulted with someone inside. After a while he returned and said: 'I'm sorry, but the *baas* says that you cannot come into this church.' Just as I reached the gate on my way out I heard someone hurrying after me. It was the deacon and he was calling me. 'What is it you want, my boy?' he asked.

'I wanted to worship in this church. But they say I cannot.'

'All right, my boy, follow me.' The deacon took me inside and led me to an isolated pew. The service began. I saw the deacon walk up to whisper something to the predikant, and immediately afterwards the doors were locked. I made up my mind to behave correctly. It just so happened that it was *Nagmaal* (Communion) and my fancy was caught by the ritual. When the collection saucers came round I prepared to give my little coin, but the official passed me. As they sang the last hymn, I rose quietly and tiptoed out. Just as I was walking down the stairs, I noticed three plainclothes men coming towards me. I hesitated. Calling me by name, one of the three men told me to follow him into a car. Inside the car a thick-set man said: 'What are you people trying to do?' I kept quiet. 'You are from *Drum*, are you not?' I remained quiet. 'I'm Major Spengler, Special Branch.' I was impressed. 'Are you a member of the African National Congress?'

'No.'

'Any other organization?'

'No. Only *Drum*.'

Another white man joined us in the car. He was asked to identify me. He scrutinized my face, then shook his head. Then an old lady from the outcoming congregation was saying, 'Where is he? Where is he? I've got to see him.' She bent down to look into the car. She looked at me and said, 'Jou Satan!'

Major Spengler instructed a police officer to take me in the car and drop me in town, 'otherwise the boys will flay him'. At the corner of Commissioner and West Streets, African Policemen were called to identify me. They ended by arguing with me about my surname, said it wasn't genuine. Then they released me.

Next day the Special Branch quizzed the Editor, asked him if he believed in apartheid! All this police action just because a Non-white wanted to go to church.

On another Saturday I again went to the Seventh Day Adventist Church. I walked through the people waiting outside the church, hoping to find somebody I could ask to allow me in. At the head of the stairs in the doorway of the church I was suddenly yanked off my feet and rushed down the steps. A big, hefty man, without even stopping to ask me to leave the church, twisted my arm behind my back and together with two others bundled me over to a waiting car. It was the 'bum's rush'. When we got to the car my huge escort pressed me sharply into it. My head struck the side and started bleeding slowly. The Editor who had been watching from the street came up to protest at my arrest by these churchgoers. He was grabbed too, and bundled into the car. The car drove off, churchmen crowded next to me. Meanwhile, our photographer made a dash for it. The last time I saw him he was taking the corner with members of the congregation chasing hot on his heels.

I was driven to Marshall Square, where I was formally charged with trespass, at the insistence of the deacon. There was no charge to bring up against the Editor, who was released. I was 'cooled off' for an hour and then released on a bail of £5, and later went to court.

But they couldn't find any charge to pin against me either, and the case was later withdrawn.

On another Sunday I went to St George's Anglican Church in Parktown. It was a beautiful church built in a lovely garden, and it had all the signs of being for 'posh' people. I walked up the garden path to the door and went in. I selected my seat. Nobody paid any attention to me, no one stared. There seemed to be nothing unusual about me being there. I still had another church to go to, so I left in about fifteen minutes. On my way out a priest asked me why I was leaving. He advised me to hurry back before all the seats were taken!

Almost every Anglican church in Johannesburg would allow me to attend. One priest said there was a special 5 a.m.(!) mass for Non-whites and it would be best not to attend a 'white' mass. Another said he wouldn't allow 'experimentation'. But one priest said: 'Why not come over for tea afterwards.' Thirteen Catholic churches gave me the Okay. Priests said: 'Yes . . . sure . . . certainly . . . you don't have to ask . . . doors open to all.'

I hurried on to the Methodist Church, Orange Grove, and walked briskly to the door. Somebody met me at the door and offered me a hymn book. I selected my seat and sat down. I was paging through the book when a man walked over threateningly to me from the front pew – then he said, 'Glad to have you with us!' There was a big Christian brotherly smile on his face, and the grip of his handshake was firm and sincere. They were trying to make something of people being 'brothers in Christ'. Their battle was a difficult one, but at least they had one thing on their side . . . the promise that man was fundamentally good.

For by one Spirit are we all baptized into one body, whether we be bond or free; and have been all made to drink into one Spirit.

CORINTHIANS 12 : 13.

NUDE PASS PARADE

Dressed men told to drop their pants

Naked. Humiliated. Hoping to God time's going to go quickly. Trying to pass off awkwardness with a shrug and wry jokes; big-shot businessmen, professional men, ordinary guys just come for a pass stand around stripped in the waiting-room of the Non-European Affairs Department in Johannesburg each work-day of the week. Hundreds of them, each day.

You want a pass. Right. You go into a structure that looks like a public convenience. It is on the corner of Albert and Polly Streets. You find a blackjack – one of those black-uniformed municipal policemen – sitting on a high stool. He barks at you that you should not be an idiot: can't you join the queue? You join the queue of hundreds of other Africans, and you get counted off.

If you are in the batch that is to see the doctor for a medical certificate, you get a little ticket that permits you to enter the eastern gate to the great building of the city's Non-European Affairs Department. You join another queue that goes in and out of iron railings and right into the building.

Inside you meet white-coated clerks and medical aids who yell you into removing your top clothing, yell you into joining a queue that leads to a green-curtained room, and yell others off from this sacrosanct queue.

In due course you get your turn to step up to the X-ray machine, hug it according to instructions, and your chest gets X-rayed. Then you pass into an inner room where you are curtly told to drop your trousers, all of you in a row.

You may be a dignified businessman, a top-class lawyer, a jeweller, a wood merchant, or anybody. You will find yourself naked. Well, you wanted a permit to work in Johannesburg, didn't you? The official world is not finicky about your embarrassed modesty.

Recently the Non-European Affairs Department issued a new instruction that all Africans who work for themselves, that is, all Africans who don't work for a European, must also be registered. This edict includes some of the elite members of African society: businessmen, doctors, musicians, lawyers, and also those who are still looking for work.

There seems to be an obvious connection with the panic over the Reef's crime wave, for many people have blamed the workless Africans for the crimes, and some of the businessmen are blamed for encouraging thefts and robberies by receiving stolen goods.

Mr John Raditsebe, of 71 Victoria Road, Sophiatown, Johannesburg, is a watchmaker. He has a little shop near the corner of Ray Street. Behind his shop are living quarters. Sometimes he has to work deep into the night to cope with the demand for his services.

Like so many others he had to go and fix his passes. He, too, had to walk the gauntlet of humiliation. 'This pass, however,' he says, 'Is so precious that one shuts one's eyes and goes through with the miserable experience.'

And there's Mr W. Lubengu, of Sophiatown, a wood merchant. Mr Rufus Khoza, of the famous Manhattan Brothers, a world-famous singer now. And more and more.

One of the most startling things that have come from this strange business is the verdict of the people affected. Terse, tired: 'Official contempt!' that is all they say.

The authorities claim that the humiliation of the mass naked parade is unavoidable. If they tried to give everyone individual attention they wouldn't have time to get through their work.

Pressed further, one official said, 'What's so wrong with this, after all? Why, during the war, old men, young men had to strip all together. They thought nothing of it.'

But, Mr Official, Mr Non-European Affairs Department, Mr Everybody who thinks things like this are OK, we aren't at war. There's no emergency. We're a civilized country, we keep telling the rest of the world.

LET THE PEOPLE DRINK

I went to a little one-room apartment in Good Street, Sophiatown, Johannesburg. It is perched in the sky like a dove-cote, and you have to go up a flight of rickety steps to get there. There was a door like a shed-door. I knocked on it, and called, 'Ousie! Ousie!' A latch screeched back, and a broad face peered at me. Then the door opened, and I stepped into a shabby passage.

I was led to a second door beyond which a drone of voices flowed. I walked into a very well-furnished, brightly-lit room. Modern jazz music of the hottest kind blared at me. And the room was crowded with African men and women sitting in clusters of threes and fours, enjoying – most of them – beer. The amber quart bottles stood all over, full, half-full, and empty. But here and there, a party was drinking brandy from tumblers measured accurately to the fourth finger.

This was the famous Little Heaven, Sophiatown's poshest shebeen.

'Hi, Can!' called the huge hostess, 'What evil plans bring you here?' Then she turned to the house at large, and announced: 'Say, folks, Can here is Mr *Drum*. Maybe you'll soon find yourselves in *Drum*.'

I grinned pointlessly. I had to, because I recognized a couple of fellows who belonged to Sophiatown's toughest gang. I didn't want them to think I was doing a story on them.

'Well, Can, what can we do for you?' asked the hostess.

'Beer,' I said.

'I got whisky, you know.'

'Yes, but beer,' I insisted.

I sat down on the studio couch, and looked around. In a corner on the bed I saw three very respectable people, two men and a woman sipping quietly from their glasses. The woman was a very well-known staff nurse. She caught my eye and smiled sweetly at me. The men turned round, and I recognized two teachers from one of Sophiatown's primary schools.

My drink came.

Half-way down my quart of beer, an African constable, cloaked in a heavy khaki-green overcoat, entered. Another one, without overcoat, followed close upon his heels. They joined me on the studio couch, and I could see the sergeant's stripes on the arm of the one with no overcoat.

Nobody turned a hair. The fellows at the table didn't even break their argument over the Freedom Charter. Our hostess waddled up to the cops. They ordered Half-a-Jack of brandy. And they paid for it!

I rose quietly, and went to say goodbye to the hostess. I still had quite a few shebeens to visit that night, and others many nights after.

In my ramblings round the shebeens of Johannesburg, I found that they were not all as comfortable and cheerful and safe as Little Heaven.

Those in the townships are of two kinds. There are the handsome, respectable ones like Little Heaven and The Sanctuary in Sophiatown, The Greenhouse in Newclare, The Kind Lady and The Gardens in Western Township, The Basement in Orlando, and Paradise in George Goch. These make you feel at home, and the atmosphere is friendly and sociable. There are kids to go and buy soda water, ginger ale, or Indian tonic for you. There is often a private room where you can sleep it off if you've had too many. These shebeens have obviously ploughed some of their profits into the business.

But there are those that are just out to make money, and damn the customer. They are dirty, and crowded, and hostile. The shebeen queen is always hurrying you to drink quickly, and swearing at somebody or other. 'You buggars act as if you've licences to drink!' She sells everything, brandy, gin, beer and skokiaan, hops, hoenene, barberton, pineapple, and even more violent concoctions. It is in these that doping takes place.

Doping is the weakening or fortifying of brandy and gin. These drinks are so precious, expensive, and difficult to come by that shebeen queens often weaken them with water, or black tea;

or dope them with tobacco water – to increase the amount or to give a quick kick.

The prices in the shebeens vary. It is safer for the house if you take it right away with you. Quite often you may get liquor below retail prices. This is because it has been stolen from a bottle-store, and the whole price is sheer profit.

But I wanted to find out where all this liquor came from. This was tough because nobody wanted to talk. Not only from fear of the police, but because shebeens don't want to give away their holes – the sources of their supplies.

My break came when a friend arranged that I should be taken along when the boys made a trip to fetch supplies for the week-end. We met in town at the corner of Diagonal and Sauer Streets. A grey van picked us up. I sat in front with the driver and my friend, and as I looked back over my shoulder, I saw two other chaps, unknown to me, sitting behind. Beyond them covering the back were a lot of flowers placed so that you could not see in when the door was open.

Nobody would tell me exactly where we were going. We travelled through by-ways and back streets for about half an hour, when we came to what appeared to be the outskirts of a town. From the registration numbers of the cars I saw, I knew that we were near Vereeniging.

Suddenly our driver swerved into a driveway and stopped be-hind of another van. He ordered us to stay where we were while he slipped into the house through a side door. We waited there for about an hour until a white man came out, completely ignored us, and went to stand where he could look up and down the street.

After a while the driver darted out of the side door and stood a moment alongside the vans, looking towards the gate. I felt that he was waiting for a signal. We were all tensely silent. Suddenly he made for the van in front of us, and opened the door at the back. The two fellows in our van clambered out through the flowers and joined him.

Then they carried out carefully packed cartons, about six of them, from the other van into ours.

'Is that the hooch?' I asked my friend.

'Mmm,' he replied, and I could hear the faint tinkle of clinking bottles. Once inside, they arranged the flowers carefully. The two chaps at the back put newspapers over the cartons and sat on two of them.

Our driver looked towards the gate, then got in, and backed slowly out. At the gate he dropped the key he had, and drove away.

'Surely that was not a bottle-store, was it?' I asked.

The driver laughed a little. 'No,' he said, 'That was not a bottle-store. That man was just a contact.'

'Ever been caught?' I wanted to know.

He laughed again. 'No. Only once the Flying Squad took a look at our flowers. That's where doing it in day-light helps.'

They dropped us at the same corner of Diagonal and Sauer Streets.

Oddly enough, most of the liquor that flows into this illicit trade does not come from Johannesburg City. It comes from suburban bottle-stores. One shebeen queen travels as far as Kimberley, in the Cape, to get it.

A usual technique is for the bottle-store owner to drive through a white suburb and note down all the vacant lots. Sometimes he collects addresses of dead people or people in gaol. By spreading it out he can enter into his books sales that do not seem too large, and still he can keep his shebeens fully supplied. Most bottle-stores do not deal with individual shebeens. They supply dealers, who in turn supply shebeens.

Another source is the big-time operators who break into bottle-stores, usually with inside help, generally a white man, who gives them the lay-out of the joint.

Several bottle-stores have been hit by the Hole-in-the-wall Gang. Their problem every time has been how to make all the noise they please in breaking through a roof or wall without attracting unwelcome attention. Someone has had to be silenced.

The wholesale merchant disposes of his liquor in one of two

ways. He may either employ a runner who sells to the shebeen, or he may have his own shebeen, where he sells the liquor.

Then there are small operators who employ white hobos to procure the liquor for them. These democratic characters visit various bottle-stores and make small purchases at each, and at the end of a day they are able to supply a runner with about six bottles of brandy. The police know about them, but there are so many of them going that it is difficult to keep track of all.

Last year about five illicit stills manufacturing brandy and beer were found on the Reef. Some of them were operated by Europeans, and some of them by Non-Europeans.

And last year, too, the cry went up, 'Let the Africans drink European Liquor!' On the whole, the police feel that their work would be considerably simplified if Africans were to be allowed light wines and beer. Many officials feel that crime would be reduced. The winegrowers are beginning to feel that the illicit trade in liquor cheats them of their fair share of the profits. And the Africans are increasingly showing their determination to get it.

The issue is no more whether Africans in general should be allowed to drink, they drink in any case. The issue is whether they may drink legally.

Prohibition has been proved impossible; there is too great a thirst for drink among the unentitled and too great a thirst for money among the bottle-store keepers. And prohibition is asking for too much from the police.

POLITICAL OFFENDERS BANNED TO THE BUSH

There has been legal argument about whether the offenders are allowed to leave the camp at all and go into the town – Mafeking, fifty miles away – on parole. It is true there are no barbed-wire fences, no armed sentries, no forced labour – and

Dr T. S. Van Rooyen, Chief Journalist of the Native Affairs Department, says that it is technically incorrect to refer to Frenchdale as a concentration camp. He explains that a removal order may be served upon any African, under Section 5 of the Native Administration Act of 1927 (which, he says, is a consolidation of all similar legislation prior to Union), if the Governor-General deems it in the public interest. Such people can be taken from any part of the Union and dumped in one small district out in the bush. They must remain there. Dr Van Rooyen says they are offered work and if incapable of it are given an allowance.

In the district of Mafeking it just so happens that these people are also offered accommodation at the camp known as Farm Frenchdale. They are not confined there, he says. In the other areas like Bushbuckridge and Vryburg, there is no such accommodation, and the people live in the district. It is only in exceptional cases, like that of people going about with sticks of dynamite, that they may be confined to a camp. 'I don't quite know what the special reasons are in the case of Mr Gwentshe, but he may be one of those exceptional cases,' concludes Dr Van Rooyen.

For Alcott Gwentshe is a man who was arrested in Mafeking on a charge of defying the Governor-General's order, and after he won his case another order was served on him, seeking to confine him to Frenchdale. But all Gwentshe carried around was his saxophone, and all he sought was a chance to keep alive within the district of Mafeking.

This Gwentshe guy with the beak nose and smart manner of a night-club compère had been, some time ago, president of the African National Congress Youth League in the Cape. In June, 1952, he led the Defiance Campaign in East London. On March 23, 1953, he was convicted under the Suppression of Communism Act with Dr Njongwe and others – fifteen in all. This was in Port Elizabeth.

On July 1, 1953, he appeared before a judge after he had been arrested, for attending a meeting when he had been banned from them. He won the case. Earlier, in May, 1953, he was visiting Tsomo, in the Transkei. Suddenly the police swooped on him. They found him in an hotel and asked him what he wanted in Tsomo. Gwentshe explained that Tsomo was his home and that he had gone there to pay his taxes. They searched him and released him. Getting arrested seems to be quite in his line, but it was not always so. Now 41, Gwentshe was born in Tsomo, but grew up in Queenstown, where he received his secondary education. Then he went to work in a shop in East London for ten years. Later he worked in a Cape Town office, in Burg Street. But he decided to open up his own shop back in East London. He hired the premises from a Mr Ngesi in Ngqika Street in Duncanville. And he was doing well. On the morning of July 19, 1954, he got a visit from the Native Commissioner at his shop. That worthy read to him an order signed by the Governor-General. The order said he should leave 'forthwith' to Bushbuckridge 800 miles away in the Eastern Transvaal. The Native Commissioner told him to leave by himself on the following day, Tuesday 20, by the Johannesburg train, and they would give him a second-class railway ticket and £2 provision money. If he failed to leave they would send a constable to escort him.

He failed to leave. He felt the time was too short, and, moreover, there was a little matter of breaking the news to his wife, Irene, dear to him for so long, and to crush a goodbye from his four sons, Mzwandile (Big Family), Mzimkulu (Big City), Zwelibanzi (Big Country), and Zweliyazuza (Land in Turmoil). But he had failed to leave. On the Wednesday they arrested him and locked him up. The following morning they escorted him to the Cambridge railway station, and no one was allowed to see him; in any case many of his friends were too scared to see him. At this place he met another chap who was also politically hot. This was Mr J. M. Lengisi. On the Johannesburg train he travelled as far as Kroonstad and was removed there. Word had come through that a crowd of people had prepared to meet him at Germiston station and give him a roof-raising ovation. So he and Lengisi were removed in cars to the Pretoria police station. 'The treatment was not bad,' Gwentshe told *Drum* with a wry smile, 'But we were photographed for the records.' Later during the same day they left with private C.I.D.s and policemen for Nelspruit, again by car. They arrived at Nelspruit, that small Eastern Transvaal town, at the dead of midnight, and slept in cells.

On Thursday 22, Lengisi was removed and taken to Barberton. Gwentshe was left for a while at Nelspruit. In the afternoon of the same Thursday he was removed by the Nelspruit police to Bushbuckridge. It all looked so thoroughly arranged. At Bushbuckridge he was taken to the Native Commissioner's office. The Native Commissioner allocated him a house near the forest and there he stayed for nine months. When he arrived he was broke – 'stone-broke, I tell you, sir' – worse still, he did not know Shangaan, the staple language of the people around there. Those people seemed to fear him. Even enlightened people would not speak to him. Life was very difficult. In fact, he was helped by two deportees from Pietersburg who had got there before him. They were Matlalas who had got into bad favour with the Government over some tribal disputes. They gave him food. He also wrote letters to his friends in East London because the Government was not supporting him. It was his friends at home who kept him alive with money for food during those nine long months. In this same period he also wrote to the East London branch of the Congress. They, too, helped with money. Later he asked his wife in East London to send him his saxophone. He used this to organize a little jazz band, and they played at functions. 'I think that's why they later deported me from there, because I was becoming socially too popular and fraternizing with too many "uncertain people".'

'My political life in that area was dormant, and I did not indulge in any politics. You see . . .' – and that wry, half-furtive smile again – 'I knew I'd be committing suicide,' Gwentshe said. So Gwentshe, the fiery leader of the Youth League, had to be dumb, had to confine his activities to soccer clubs and his pet jazz band. And that was just as well, for in April, 1955, some C.I.D.s came from Roodepoort and went around Bushbuckridge asking questions about him from the people who hired his band, which he called the Bushbuckridge Band. They were not satisfied that he only played Bushbuckridge Blues, so they went to see the secretary of a local football club and asked more questions. They wanted to know if the secretary knew Gwentshe, and what private and political activities he exercised in his leisure. But those local fellows were only interested in Gwentshe as a musician. That, too, apparently was not good enough. As it happened, Gwentshe was teaching a young boy of promising talent to play the saxophone; they would meet a couple of times a week for practices. One day, police from the Native Affairs Department paid the boy a visit. They asked him some questions. All Gwentshe ever knew about it was that the boy became too scared to come to rehearsals again.

Gwentshe was called to the Native Affairs Department and served with a further banishment order which said that by 1 p.m. that day he should be ready to leave the place, and make a 500 mile move to Frenchdale in the Mafeking district.

So at about ten minutes to one he left Bushbuckridge with two escorts. When they arrived in Johannesburg they took their luggage to the cloakroom. His escorts had never been in Johannesburg before and he had to show them the cloakroom, and the booking-office for the trip to Mafeking. From there they left for Mafeking, where he had to see the Native Commissioner. That official told Gwentshe that he did not like people like him there, but that he was just forced to carry out the orders of the Government. He also said that he had a place for him to stay, in town, until Monday, May 9. This was Friday, May 6.

So Gwentshe was placed in a Native Affairs depot where they kept Nyasalanders who were illegal immigrants, on condition that he did not talk to anybody. Gwentshe wanted to know if he wanted water or relief, should he not ask anybody? The Commissioner said even if he wanted water he should not speak to anybody. Gwentshe replied, 'I promise, though I'm not sure. And by what authority do you say that? Even Swart, the Minister of Justice, bans us from public gatherings, but he never says I shouldn't speak to anyone.' The Native Commissioner got angry and removed him to Frenchdale forthwith in his car with some policemen. At Frenchdale the Commissioner showed him his two huts and left immediately. When he opened one of the huts he noticed it was not ready for human habitation. It was dirty and so empty that there was not even a bucket. The other hut was worse, with its broken windows. Now, in Mafeking when the Commissioner had got angry with Gwentshe's cheeky answers they had left so soon that Gwentshe did not get a chance to buy supplies. He found the place 'a desert', as he puts it. There was no shop, no post office, not a cow, not even a mealie stalk that nature might have allowed to grow accidentally. The nearest village was Pitsani, about 12 miles away. He went round the other huts. There was Thompson Dlamini, exiled ex-Induna from Bergville in Natal. Dlamini helped him with food which he had scraped together by devious ingenuity, and then they talked and talked.

He stayed there through the Friday and Saturday. On Sunday the Native Commissioner came with a police lieutenant from Mafeking to arrest people supposed to be staying in the camp when they were not exiles. Gwentshe spoke to him about the state of his hut. The Commissioner said there was nothing he could do about it. So Gwentshe asked to be allowed to go to town to buy beds, stoves, pots and groceries; and to write to East London. The Commissioner gave leave to visit the Mafeking shops. Gwentshe wrote to East London, and to the Governor-General (Supreme Chief of all the Africans). He described to the Governor-General his conditions in Frenchdale: that he could find no work since he was not allowed into Mafeking; that he had no support; that he was in what was virtually a desert; and that he could not even use his saxophone because there were no people there amongst whom he could organize functions. The Governor-General replied that he would see the Cabinet. Since then, about May 11, 1955, he has heard nothing further about it all. 'I don't know what the Cabinet decided on the matter,' he remarked bitterly. When the Native Commissioner had taken him into Mafeking he told Gwentshe to stay in the same old Native Affairs Depot. Gwentshe started complaining about the filthy condition of the place and the stinking blankets. The Native Commissioner was very sympathetic. He explained that he had no other place else he would help him. But he just had to keep him there.

For quite a while no money came from East London. Gwentshe had so little money that furniture was out of the question. It was hard even to pay his way back to Frenchdale. He was completely stranded, and soon there was not even the money to eat. He appealed to the Native Commissioner, who gave him some money. 'Out of my own pocket,' he said. First £1 10s., and later 10s.

'I think the man had suddenly appreciated the seriousness of my plight,' Gwentshe explained, 'for he was most sympathetic.' But Gwentshe had to fend for himself somehow. There was his horn, and there were a few fellows who looked as if they could distinguish one note from another, and make a few new ones. He organized a small band again. They rehearsed in the Mafeking Stad and the Location. Soon they were playing at parties and dances, and they made a little money – barely enough to keep the wolf from the door. In February 1956, their band was hired to play at the reception of the new, young Barolong chief, Kebalepile Montsioa, in Mafeking. Naturally, the Native Commissioner and other officials of the Native Affairs Department were present. And there was Gwentshe moaning into the saxophone. He was arrested and kept in custody for three days. 'The police did not tell me the charge,' Gwentshe wailed. 'When I wanted to know the charge, the police said: *Sluit hom op!* (Lock him up!)'

Luckily a friend, Dr S. Molema, paid the bail of £25 for him. The case was scheduled to appear on February 29. It was again remanded to March 14. Advocate Joe Slovo came from Johannesburg to defend him. The charge was the defiance of the Governor-General's order by not staying in Frenchdale. During cross-examination by Adv. Joe Slovo, the Native Commissioner admitted that he had lost his friendliness towards Gwentshe after he had visited East London and had been influenced by the Native Commissioner there. The defence also argued that the Commissioner had promised to get Gwentshe a job in Pitsani, and that proved that Gwentshe could stay anywhere as long as it was in the district of Mafeking. Gwentshe won the case. Meanwhile, he has applied to the Supreme Court to have the banishment order set aside. But he dreams . . . he still can dream, this man.

'Look here, Gwentshe,' I said to him during one of his visits to Mafeking, 'I'd like to see this Frenchdale place. It's all very well to say the Government has a concentration camp for political offenders, but where's the evidence?'

When we got there Gwentshe took us to the leader of the camp. He is Mr Kuena who describes himself as 'the important Divine servant in the Divine activities'. Indeed when we got to his hut a 'Divine service' was just beginning. His pretty daughter, Aletta, and some girls from Mahelo around, were yelling their heads off, Zion-fashion. We were invited into the 'service' and found Bishop Kuena's brother conducting it.

Then spoke P. Tsepho K. Mokwena – he wears a khaki uniform and a moustache that curls with his speech and makes him appear snarling – he said, 'We have sent out the sorry story of our condition here many times, but we never knew whether the people were aware of this barren existence. Let them get it.' Mokwena was sent to Frenchdale from Witzieshoek in 1954. He was deported for refusing to cull his cattle and to repair a fence that had been torn down during the riots there. He says the authorities declared him dangerous when he tried to express his opinion on cattle culling.

Old Thompson Dlamini could hardly bide his turn to speak. He stood up dramatically and raising his arms, he said, 'God brought you here. God has heard our prayers, and has come among us. You see us in trouble, without food, in ramshackle houses that look like bird's nests. How can the Government say they don't care about us? A Government is a provider, one that cares for his people, even his prisoners. If the Government will not do that, he is no Government . . .' Then he veered off into a praise of Tshaka, 'Thou bird that devourest the lesser birds in the morning, and when the morrow cometh, thou devourest more . . .' It was aggressive. Dlamini is an ex-Induna from Bergville, Natal, but is not connected at all with the dagga raids there this year, for he came to the camp in 1953. He was an Induna of the Vunamina tribe, and supporter of Chief Vunamina. The Native Commissioner, whom Dlamini says the people at Bergville called Nyamazan (Wild Beast), and the late Dr Ka I. Seme were plotting to oust Vunamina in favour of Bangeni, the present chief. When Vunamina got married to a daughter of the late King Solomon ka Dinizulu, the tribe agreed to pay the *lobola* (bride-price) of 110 cattle. 'I was one of at least sixty people who paid the *lobola*,' Dlamini says, 'at a time when Vunamina had fallen from favour with the authorities. But I alone was deported. Fifty-nine others are still back there. I even asked the Commissioner why he had left the fifty-nine behind. He said, "That's my decision, don't ask questions"'.

Now, oddly, Thompson Dlamini cheerfully accepts his position. 'I am a man with two farms: one in Natal and one here,' he said, and roared with laughter. He has actually brought out his fourth and youngest wife, Lena, and her seventeen-month-old child, Mafeking (that is the child's name), to come to stay with him.

The only other man who has brought out his family is Matela Mantsoe. He spoke with real bitterness. 'They brought us here without a trial,' he screeched. 'They do not try our case. This is the first time for me to hear of a prison that has no food, no water, no hope of release. At home my stuff is rotting. My grocery store is rotting. Here – here –' and he held up a colourful Basotho blanket with rat-eaten holes in it – 'That is how my property is rotting at home. This, my wife just brought to me to show me.' And he broke into terrible bitter tears.

Matela Mantsoe is also from the Witzieshoek area. He was closely related to the great chiefs of Witzieshoek, and had been at Frenchdale for about four years. He seemed to be in a daze about the exact events that went before his deportation. It was obvious he shied from thinking about them.

When Bishop Kuena called on Gwentshe to speak, Gwentshe startled us off our stools by just barking, '*Mayibuye!*' There was a long, deep silence before we walked outside the huts. I examined them from the outside. They were sturdily built of concrete blocks with thatched roofs. Each deportee had two allocated to him, and they stood in two rows, leaving a wide space between. Some occupants had tried to make little front-yards or gardens, and in the back the ground had been scratched here and there. I saw a calf or two grazing around, but it was promptly explained to me that they belonged to Mahelo people who sometimes allowed the deportees to milk their cows. As we left the camp, Gwentshe sadly said, 'You leave the place sadder and quieter than it was.'

IV

ENDINGS

'MR DRUM': HENRY NXUMALO

February, 1957

One Saturday afternoon Henry Nxumalo, the News Editor of *Golden City Post*, set out to Sophiatown to look for me. He didn't find me in. He came three times, but still didn't find me in; curse my roving ways! Then he went to see another reporter friend, Bloke Modisane, and chatted with him into the early evening. Bloke thought that it was getting late, what with the boys outside getting so knife-happy these days, and he urged Henry to go home early, or to stay for the night. But Henry explained that he had a job to do in Newclare, and proposed to go and sleep at his cousin Percy Hlubi's house in Western Township. So at about 7 o'clock in the evening, Henry left the 'Sunset Boulevard' – Bloke's home in Sophiatown, and went to Western Township, across the rails.

He must have felt disgracefully dry, because those days just after Christmas were arid and desert-like in the Western Areas. A man just couldn't find a drop. Henry got to Percy's house, and explained to Percy and his wife that he would like to pass the night there. However, he would first like to go to Newclare where he had a job to do. He would return later to sleep. Meanwhile, the men sat talking, whilst the woman prepared a bed for Henry. Before she turned in for the night, she told Henry that when he came back he would probably find them asleep; he shouldn't bother to knock; just open the door and go to bed.

Percy looked at the time and noticed that it was close on 11 o'clock. He told Henry to postpone his trip to Newclare for the following day. It was so awfully late. 'Never put off for tomorrow what you can do today,' Henry back-fired, grinning. Then he rose and walked out into the warm night. He never came back to the bed prepared for him.

The following morning, Mrs Hlubi rose early to go to work in Krugersdorp. She was a nurse there and she normally took her train at Westbury Station. She set out for work at about a quarter past five that Sunday morning. When she got to the spot where Malotane Street flowed out of Ballenden Avenue like a tributary, she noticed a body lying on the green grass, one shoe off, one arm twisted behind, the head pressed against the ground, the eyes glazed in sightless death. There were bloody wounds all over the head and body. Good heavens, it was Henry Nxumalo! In hysterical frenzy she rushed back home to tell her husband. Percy went to the scene and saw the battered body of his cousin. He got his friend, Mr Vil-Nkomo, to inform Henry's employer. He contacted the police. He chartered a car to go and tell Henry's wife – most cheerless of tasks. Then he got someone to go round and tell all the *Drum* boys.

The way I got the news was through the wife of Benjamin Gwigwi Mrwebi. Gwigwi himself was away in Durban with his combo, the Jazz Dazzlers. So Salome, his wife, took it upon herself to inform those of us who were around. She found me still in bed lazing luxuriously after 8 o'clock, and she broke the news to me. Stunned, I crawled out of bed and went with her to the spot marked X. There was already a little crowd gathered and from all the streets flowing into Ballenden people were streaming to the spot.

There he lay, the great, gallant Henry Nxumalo, who had fought bravely to bare cruelty, injustice, and narrow-mindedness; there he lay in the broiling sun, covered by two flimsy rags.

He who had accepted the challenge of life and dedicated himself against the wrongs of mankind, now lay on the roadside, his last battlefield the gutter, his last enemies arrant knaves for whom even Henry had raised his trumpet call. And there was a staggered trail of bloody footsteps that told the graphic story of that night's drama.

The unknowing still ask, who was this Henry Nxumalo?

Henry was born thirty-nine years ago in Port Shepstone, the eldest of seven children.

Because their parents died when they were still young, they more or less had to look after themselves. This one fact accounts for the independent spirit in Henry and his surviving brothers. Henry went to school at St Francis, Mariannhill, and did his Junior Certificate, but while he was doing Matric, his father died and he had to abandon school. He took up a job as a kitchen boy in Durban, but left it because he didn't like it. He came to Johannesburg and found a job in a boilermaker's shop. In his spare time he wrote poetry for the *Bantu World.*

Later he got a job with the *Bantu World* as a messenger and hung on for three years until he became sports editor. When the war came he joined up and became a sergeant. He went up North and made various friends. The world beyond showed him how other people thought and lived and when he came back he was a frustrated man. He came back to the *Bantu World* and made extra money by writing for a Negro paper, the *Pittsburgh Courier*. In 1946 he married a young nurse called Florence. He then left to work on a gold mine, later doing welfare work for the British Empire Service League, while still free-lancing for European papers. In 1951 he joined *Drum.*

It was in 1952 that the fabulous character of 'Mr *Drum*' was created. First the idea was a stunt whereby Mr *Drum* would disguise himself and walk through the locations. The first person who could identify him with a copy of *Drum* won a £5-note. Up to his death many people were still trying to earn a fiver off Henry.

But the idea of a 'Mr *Drum*' had tremendous possibilities. The first opportunity came with the famous Bethal story. Farmers were rumoured to be ill-treating their labourers in the Bethal district and Henry was sent over as a labourer himself to investigate. He came back with a story that shook the whole country. 'Mr *Drum* Goes to Bethal' was the first Mr *Drum* exposure. And from there Henry had set *Drum* on the map.

Henry got himself arrested on the slight offence of not having a night pass, and he went to jail. His experiences in jail made a chilling story that caused an international sensation. Just about this time a friend of mine reading the story in *Drum* said to me, 'This Mr *Drum* fellow is going bang into history.'

He regarded himself as a contemporary social historian.

Why the bloody hell did they have to choose him to murder? I cannot hide my bitterness at all. But, dear Henry, Mr *Drum* is not dead. Indeed, even while you lived, others were practising the game of Mr *Drum*. Now, we shall take over where you left off. We want you, as you look down on us from among the angels, to mutter, 'The boys sure make a good job of that game, and looks like they might get the world a little cleaner from what I left it.' Bye now.

THE BOY WITH THE TENNIS RACKET

Someone had passed the buck to me. The story went out that a razor-sharp journalist from Durban was coming to Johannesburg to work in our main office. The editor had told someone to find accommodation for him, and that someone had decided that his initiation was best in my hands. In those days handing an other-town boy into my hands for initiation was subtlest excruciation. Not that we would persecute him, we only sought to divest him of the naïvetés and extraneous moralities with which we knew he would be encumbered.

He came, I remember, in the morning with a suitcase and a tennis racket – ye gods, a tennis racket! We stared at him. The chaps on *Drum* at that time had fancied themselves to be poised on a dramatic, implacable kind of life. Journalism was still new to most of us and we saw it in the light of the heroics of Henry Nxumalo, decidedly not in the light of tennis, which we classed with draughts.

He had a puckish, boyish face, and a name something like Nathaniel Nakasa. We soon made it Nat. I took him to Sophiatown and showed him the room where he would stay – what was it? Three minutes, five minutes? Then I took him to my shebeen in Edith Street.

There was a beautiful girl there, and I hoped Nat would make her. As a matter of cold fact, as he declined drink after drink, I decided that he was interested. She was Tswana and he Zulu, but they got on swimmingly, love being polyglot. Honest, I don't know how it happened, but I left him there. He told me later, that a few *tsotsis* came in and he approached them with trepidated terror. He asked them if they knew where Can Themba lived and they immediately looked hostile. (At first, they thought he contemplated some harm to the revered Can Themba.) But when Mpho, the girl, explained that this was really a friend of the chap, who had deserted him there in one of his drunken impulses, they said, 'O.K. Durban-boy, hang around and we'll take you there'.

This is a measure of Nat's character. He was in a new situation. He knew about Jo'burg tsotsis, the country's worst. He was scared – he told me later he was. But he went with them, chatted with them, wanted to know what type of character this, his host, was. Though he got only grunts, it was the journalist in action, not the terrified fish out of water.

He found me at home, out of this world's concerns. Later, he found out about Jo'burg without the aid of my derelictions. He quickly learned about the united nations of Fordsburg and Malay Camp; about the liberal enclaves in Hillbrow; about the cosmopolitanism of Johannesburg. Also about the genuine values in those people who were not trying to prove or protest anything: God knows South Africa begs any stranger to want to prove or protest something, and Johannesburg is its Mecca.

But Nat sought for something inside himself that would make language with the confused environment in which he now existed. He sought, fought, struggled, argued, posed – but I doubt if he found it. The South African stubbornacy was too much for him, and he had to go into exile.

The bitterest commentary on South Africa is typified by Nat. All those Africans who want to be loyal, hard-working, intelligent citizens of the country are crowded out. They don't wa bleach themselves, but they want to participate and contribute to the wonder that that country can become. They don't want to be fossilized into tribal inventions that are no more real to them than they would have been real to their forefathers.

Nat's was such a voice. Sobukwe's is that of protest and resistance. Casey Motsisi's that of derisive laughter. Bloke Modisane's that of implacable hatred. Ezekiel Mphahlele's that of intellectual contempt. Nimrod Mkele's that of patient explanation to be patient. Mine, that of self-corrosive cynicism. But Nat told us, 'There must be humans on the other side of the fence; it's only we haven't learned how to talk'.

We replied, 'Humans? Not enough.'

One day, we met at a dry cleaners called the Classic. Nat bought the drinks and said he had an idea. Ideas were sprouting all over the place, but any excuse for a drink was good enough.

After the ninth we got around to discussing the idea. Nat proposed starting a really good, artistic magazine. He wanted all of us – I don't mean just those Non-White journalists present – but all of us: Black, White, Coloured, Indian. For want of superior inspiration we decided to call the damned thing *The Classic* – the place where it was conceived, born, and most of the time bred. Most of us got stinkingly drunk, but Nat captained the boat with a level head and saw to it that we met dead-line.

He slipped into the artistic-intellectual set of Hillbrow and I had to go there. In between he met a girl who seemed to match the accomplishments he sought. She was African (that would vindicate him from the slur that any White woman was better than every Black woman, though I think Nat would have thought of this with contempt; she was educated and intelligent (though I think Nat was no snob); she was lively and interesting (though I think Nat would have none of a floozie); she could mix with the High, the Middle and the Low (Nat chose what he wanted from High, Middle and Low). Eventually, she eclipsed herself and went to marry someone in Europe.

Nat had a brother here in Swaziland, Joe Nakasa. One day Joe took me to Chesterville in Durban to meet his family.

There was a father, a sister and a brother. Another brother was in England studying at Cambridge. Their mother was in Sterkfontein Mental Hospital, unable to recognize even her sons. Nat talked little about his mother, but once when I had gone there with him, he broke out into bitter, scalding tears. I had not been there when he saw his mother, but I guessed that it was a gruelling, cruel experience.

Then he went to America. We thought this was the big break.*

At the time of his death, Nat was planning interesting things, journalistically speaking, interesting things . . .

Quo Vadis.

**In the special obituary number of* The Classic *in which this article appeared, the Editor wrote: 'In 1964 he was granted a Niemann Scholarship for study at Harvard University, but his passport was withheld. He left South Africa toward the end of 1964 on an exit permit which prohibited his return to this country. He was twenty-eight years old when he died on the 14th of July, 1965, after a fall from the seventh storey of a building in New York.'*

REQUIEM FOR SOPHIATOWN

Realism can be star-scattering, even if you have lived your whole unthinking life in reality. Especially in Sophiatown, these days, where it can come with the sudden crash of a flying brick on the back of your head.

Like the other day when Bob Gosani and I sneaked off towards our secret shebeen in Morris Street. We were dodging an old friend of ours whom we call the Leech, for he is one of those characters who like their drink – any amount – so long as someone else pays for it.

Well, this secret shebeen in Morris Street was a nice place. You take a passage through Meyer Street over haphazard heaps of bricks where houses have been broken down, you find another similar passage that leads you from Ray Street into Edith Street, where you find another passage, neater, having always been there between the Coloured School and Jerusalem-like slum-houses, you go down a little, and suddenly there it is.

Quite a fine place, too. A little brick wall, a minute garden of mostly Christmas flowers, a half-veranda (the other half has become a little kitchen) with the floor of the veranda polished a bright green.

Inside, the sitting-room may be cluttered with furniture, it is so small, but you sink comfortably into a sofa as one of the little tables that can stand under the other's belly is placed before you, and you make your order. Half-a-jack of brandy!

How often have Bob and I not whooped happily, 'Yessus! the Leech will never find us here'. So, though there were more direct routes to this place, we always took the passages. They say these people can smell when you are going to take a drink.

But that day, as we emerged into Morris Street, it was as if that brick had just struck us simultaneously on our heads. That sweet little place was just not there. Where it should have been was a grotesque, grinning structure of torn red brick that made it look like the face of a mauled boxer trying to be sporting after his gruel. A nausea of despair rose up in me, but it was Bob who said the only appropriate thing:

'Shucks.'

Here is the odd thing about Sophiatown. I have long been inured to the ravages wreaked upon it; I see its wrecks daily, and through many of its passages that have made such handy short-cuts for me, I have stepped gingerly many times over the tricky rubble. Inside of me, I have long stopped arguing the injustice, the vindictiveness, the strong-arm authority of which prostrate Sophiatown is a loud symbol.

Long ago I decided to concede, to surrender to the argument that Sophiatown was a slum, after all. I am itchingly nagged by the thought that slum-clearance should have nothing to do with the theft of freehold rights. But the sheer physical fact of Sophiatown's removal has intimidated me.

Moreover, so much has gone – veritable institutions. Fatty of the Thirty-nine Steps, now, that was a great shebeen! It was in Good Street. You walked up a flight of steps, the structure looked dingy as if it would crash down with you any moment. You opened a door and walked into a dazzle of bright electric light, contemporary furniture, and massive Fatty. She was a legend. Gay, friendly, coquettish, always ready to sell you a drink. And that mama had everything: whisky, brandy, gin, beer, wine – the lot. Sometimes she could even supply cigars. But now that house is flattened. I'm told that in Meadowlands she has lost the zest for the game. She has even tried to look for work in town. Ghastly.

There was Dwarf, who used to find a joke in everything. He used to walk into Bloke's place and catch us red-handed playing the music of Mozart. He used to cock his ear, listen a little and in his gravel voice comment, 'No wonder he's got a name like that'. There was nothing that Dwarf loved more than sticking out his tongue to a cop and running for it. I once caught him late at night in his Meadowlands house washing dishes! He still manfully tries to laugh at himself.

And Mabeni's, where the great Dolly Rathebe once sang the blues to me. I didn't ask her; she just sidled over to me on the couch and broke into song. It was delicious. But now Dolly is in Port Elizabeth, and Mabeni, God knows where.

These are only highlights from the swarming, cacophonous, strutting, brawling, vibrating life of the Sophiatown that was. But it was not all just shebeeny, smutty, illegal stuff. Some places it was the stuff that dreams are made of.

I am thinking of those St Cyprian's schoolboys who, a decade ago, sweatingly dug out the earth behind the house of the Community of the Resurrection, in order to have a swimming pool. It still stands, and the few kids left still paddle in it. Some of those early schoolboys of St Cyprian's later went up to Father Ross or Father Raynes or Father Huddleston who wangled a bursary for them to go to St Peter's, then on to Fort Hare, and later even Wits, to come back doctors.

Their parents, patiently waiting and working in town, skimped a penny here, a tickey there, so that they might make the necessary alterations to their house, or pay off the mortgage. And slowly Sophiatown was becoming house-proud.

Of course, there were pressures too heavy for them. After the war, many people came to Johannesburg to seek for work and some hole to night in. As they increased they became a housing problem. As nobody seemed to care, they made Sophiatown a slum.

But the children of those early Sophiatonians – some of them – are still around. It is amazing how many of them are products of the Anglican Mission at St Cyprian's. I meet them often in respectable homes, and we talk the world to tatters.

Mostly we talk of our lot in life. After all, too often we have been told that we are the future leaders of our people. We are the young stalwarts who are supposed to solve the problems of our harassed world.

'Not political unity, we need,' one would say; 'Our society is too diverse and unwieldy for that. Just a dynamic core of purified fighters with clear objectives and a straightforward plan of action. That is all.'

Another, 'No! We must align ourselves with the new forces at play in Africa today. There is already the dynamicity. The idea of a one Africa has never been put as powerfully as at Accra recently. You see, Africans, wherever they are, have not a territorial, a local loyalty: they don't feel that they belong to a South Africa, or a Federation, or a Tanganyika, or a Kenya, or a West Africa; but with Africans in the whole of Africa. In fact, many of us are wondering if Arabs and Egyptians are also Africans. They probably are.'

Still another, 'But if the boys in the North are getting busy, shouldn't we start something here ourselves?'

'Waal, you see, our ANC here has been caught with its pants down. The Africanists are claiming that Accra has proclaimed their stand. And the ANC representative there could only discuss the tactical difficulties of the ANC in South Africa with her special conditions.'

'Ya. But this African Personality idea, what does it mean to us? What does it mean, anyway?'

'I'll tell you. In the world today are poised against each other two massive ideologies: of the East and of the West. Both of them play international politics as if we're bound to choose between them. Between them only. We have just discovered that we can choose as we like, if we grow strong in our own character. But there's more to this. The West has had a damned long time to win us. Win us over to Western thinking. Western Christian way of living. Their ideas of democracy and their Christian ideals were wonderful, but they did not mean them.

'Let me explain. We are quite a religious people. We accept the idealism of Christianity. We accept its high principles. But in a stubborn, practical sense we believe in reality. Christian Brotherhood must be real. Democracy must actually be the rule of the people: not of a white hobo over a black M.A.

'To us, if a witchdoctor says he'll bring rain, we not only want to see the rain fall, but also see the crops sprout from the earth. That's what a rainmaker's for, nay? If the bone-thrower says he'll show up the bastard who's been slinging lightning at me, I expect him to swing that bolt of lightning right back. So if the priest says God's on my side, I'd like to see a few more chances and fewer whiteman's curses.

'But, in any case, Christianity is now an anaemic religion. It cannot rouse the ancient in me – especially the Chaka instinct I still have. Now, you and I are educated guys. We don't go for the witchcraft stuff. And we don't want to go for the juke-box stuff. But much as we deny it, we still want the thrill of the wild blood of our forefathers. The whites call it savagery. Ineradicable barbarism. But in different degrees we want the colour, and vigour and vibrant appeal of it all. So the *tsotsi* seeks in the cowboy the way to strut across the streets with swaying hips and a dangerous weapon in each hand. So the zionist thumps his drum and gyrates his holy fervour up the streets. So you and I and these guys here discuss politics, teasingly dancing around the idea of violence.

'All it means is that in wanting to express her demand for

democratic self-determination, Africa is also releasing her ancien most desire to live life over the brim. That's how come we sometimes seem to talk in two voices.'

'Wait a minute,' another shrieks, 'Wait a minute. We're not all like that. Some of us would like to get things right, and start anew. Some piece of social engineering could get things working right, if our moral purposes were right, not just vengeful.'

'Sure, but our masters have taught this damned thing violence so well by precept – often practice – that they get you to believe that it's the only way to talk turkey to them.'

We do not talk about this particular subject only; our subjects are legion. Nkrumah must be a hell of a guy, or is he just bluffing? What about our African intellectuals who leave the country just when we need them most? But is it honestly true that we don't want to have affairs with white girls? What kind of white supremacy is this that cannot stand fair competition? What will happen if a real topmost Afrikaner Nationalist gets caught by the Immorality Act? In fact, all those cheeky questions that never get aired in public.

But it always ends up with someone saying, 'Aw shut up, folks, you got no plan to liberate us.'

Somewhere here, and among a thousand more individualistic things, is the magic of Sophiatown. It is different and itself. You don't just find your place here, you make it and you find yourself. There's a tang about it. You might now and then have to give way to others making their ways of life by methods which aren't in the book, but you can't be bored. You have the right to listen to the latest jazz records at Ah Sing's over the road. You can walk a Coloured girl of an evening down to the Odin Cinema, and no questions asked. You can try out Rhugubar's curry with your bare fingers without embarrassment. All this with no sense of heresy. Indeed, I've shown quite a few white people 'the little Paris of the Transvaal' – but only a few were Afrikaners.

What people have thought to be the brazen-ness of Sophiatown has really been its clean-faced frankness. And, of course, its swart jowl against the rosy cheek of Westdene.

Ay, me. That was the Sophiatown that was.

I shall have to leave these respectable homes of my friends and stumble over the loose bricks back to my den. I hear tell that Blackie is still about in his shack behind the posh house in devastated Millar Street.

Blackie's landlord is still facing it out, what the hell for? Since the Rathebe case most of the standholders have decided to capitulate. They are selling out like rats letting the passengers sink. Solly got caught in this – the newest racket. His landlord told him nothing. Waited for him to pay the next month's rent, although he knew that he was planning to sell out. The Resettlement Board has been very sympathetic with such cases; it has told tenants not to pay rent to the landlords any more, for they may suddenly be given yesterday's notice and the G.G. will come to break down the house over their heads.

Solly was not at home when the landlord trekked. When he got there he found his furniture was left outside and a policeman was guarding the house. Poor Solly had to rush about looking for some place to put his stuff for the night. Half-a-dozen friends helped.

And still I wander among the ruins trying to find one or two of the shebeens that Dr Verwoerd has overlooked. But I do not like the dead-eyes with which some of these ghost houses stare back at me. One of these days I, too, will get me out of here. Finish and clear!

THE BOTTOM OF THE BOTTLE

Comes a time when a man feels that everything in his personal organization cannot go on as before for much longer. No dramatic decision may be taken in some bursting hour of change. But all the same, a man may feel that those in their bits